Th

GW00385125

THE SECRETS

OF

BEACON COURT

BY

LOTTA VOKES

Lotta Vokes

The Secrets of Beacon Court

A story written by eleven neighbours and
friends each in turn adding their chapter to what
had gone before; an amusing device to throttle the
utter boredom
of the Covid 19 lockdown of 2021.

Copyright 20/21 Charlotte Vokes
ISBN 9798717150781
Amazon Edition

Lotta Vokes

This book is dedicated to all who suffered under the devastating viral pandemic of 2020 and 2021

Per auxilium aliis auxilium tibi

MOTTO OF THE CARTHUSIAN FAMILY

(Help yourself by helping others)

Lotta Vokes

PREFACE

Situated at the top end of a winding road high on the shoulder of Carrick Gollen, with a commanding view of vessels approaching or departing Dublin port, Beacon Court was more than well placed for its owner, Edward Carthusian, to keep an eye on the movement of his three masted ships, laden with cargo or ballast, as they sailed in or out of Dublin port at the start or finish of their journeys to and from Jamaica. Ships that made him lots of money.

When he had his eye glued to his new toy, a 36-inch Baines and Blunt telescope, and he spotted one of his ships out by Bray Head, he would get Beacon Court's gardener/handyman to fire off a distress rocket; a beacon light to let the ship's master know he had been seen ... a friendly welcome to ships on the final leg of their journey home, a God's Speed farewell to those departing.

But the telescope did not just follow the movement of his vessels, oh no, it also gave Carthusian a chance to monitor progress being made on the building of similar sized mansion to his own in the village of Old Connaught, three hundred feet or so below him. It was going to be an imposing structure too, especially if the owner added the extra embellishment of a twenty-foot canopy, supported by an ionic colonnade, which it was a widely known he was considering, a rival and imposing gentleman's seat if ever there was one.

Tragically, while the builders of Old Connaught House were still applying the finishing the touches to their work, the owner, Lewis Robert, unexpectedly died and the completed, but never occupied house, was put on the market.

The unlikely purchaser was the Archbishop of Dublin. He and his family held possession of it for four generations until it was sold to a religious institution in the late sixties.

Twenty years later it was bought by a building developer. He dismantled the interior and, while preserving as many of the original features as he could possibly manage, he converted what remained into apartments which were then sold. That was in the 2000s. Presently, enlarged and enhanced by its re-generated garden, Old Connaught House is at the start of a new life.

Beacon Court was following Old Connaught House on an uncannily similar path of conversion when the twin daughters of its current owner, Rory Carthusian, the three times great grandson of Edward Carthusian who had built it, altered it in a similar way. The situation in that house had arisen in consequence of Rory's tragic early onset of dementia, a disastrous situation which had led to him being moved permanently into a nursing home, leaving his twin, thoroughly irresponsible, daughters in charge. It might not have been such an issue if his wife, Kate, had still been alive, but she had died in in a freak accident six years earlier, when a car's front tyre blew out and the un-steerable vehicle mounted the pavement in Bray Main Street, pinning her to the wall of the Royal Hotel.

The Secrets of Beacon Court

With their father well out of the way, the twin girls Angela and Mitzi, in their thirties, each took possession of half the accommodation in Beacon Court and brought in their boyfriends - Ambrose Finnegan and Jimmy Hennessey. Everybody else in the wider family was disgusted at their insensitivity. It was the end of an era. Where there had been order, there was going to be chaos. Where there had been harmony, conflict loomed. The girls had always been bound together by that amazing and mysterious force that ties twin together. But, when the boys moved in, that all broke down and the girls' attachment to their men quickly became greater than their attachment to each other.

Such disharmony might have been assuaged if the boys had got on with each other … but they did not; they argued over everything, but especially over money. They had no jobs … why waste time working when the Carthusians had plenty of loot to spare … or so it had seemed.

The girls did not have jobs either, they had never needed one. The four of them spent their time with friends who were equally devoid of social responsibility and common sense. To put it in its starkest terms, their lives were being propelled by engines that had almost run out of fuel. Realisation of the perilous situation they were heading for eventually brought a temporary ceasefire in the wars the four of them were having with each other and bought time for them to plot their way out of their difficulties. The solution they came up with turned out to be copying what was going on in Old Connaught House; a conversion into an apartment complex.

The two largest units the girls reserved for themselves and their lovers, while the rest were leased out at rents that would (by their calculations), enable them to avoid their reckless style of living being in the slightest impeded. Ambrose and Jimmy occupied themselves with 'managing' the apartment complex for the girls, with most of the actual work, as is usual in such cases, being contracted out. But one thing they made absolutely sure about was to collect the rents from the tenants themselves.

It had taken nearly two years to set it all up, and now, four years on, what a disaster it was proving to be. Downstairs, the two 'three bed 'apartments flanking the library, which doubled as an entrance hall, were taken by Angela and Ambrose, and Mitzi and Jimmy; while Effie Boyle, a widow; the first to move into the reshuffled accommodation, took the east facing 'two bed' that lay between them. Upstairs all four apartments had two bedrooms and they were occupied by Kitty Rae, a retired actress; Sean Salinger, a young and highly successful investment portfolio manager (or so he said); Geraldine Haven, a retired solicitor who had spent most of her working life in the Department of Justice ... and Peter Portius, a bull of a man;a big, ignorant, and thoroughly unpleasant individual, who had just retired from the South African customs service and was said to have distant relations living nearby. On the face of it, ironically, one might have assumed Beacon Court was a settled and friendly community, but anyone inclined to take such a view would be a long way from what knowing what was really going on ... and it

The Secrets of Beacon Court

was not harmony or 'good will to all men'. Oh no … life in Beacon Court was a battle; a battle that appeared to be unending; one with some odd twists and turns … as they soon found out!

It was Bunty McGilligan, the twice weekly, ten euro an hour, cleaner; a woman who had put more working hours into Beacon Court than any other living person, who discovered him.

He was lying on the library floor, face down, with a dark trickle of drying blood coming from somewhere beneath his left ear. Beside him, a dark green leather-bound book lay open … it seemed to be written in what looked like Japanese.

CHAPTER ONE

Bunty's first thought was that he was drunk, it certainly would not be unusual, but it was a bit early at 9 a.m. She had seen a lot in her time in this house, but had opted to pass no comment on what she saw and heard. Bunty's surprise turned to shock and horror though, when she bent down to help him up and realised that he was beyond it.

He was not breathing, was he? He could he be dead? What was she to do?

She heard a noise, a door closing upstairs and called out 'Help me somebody. Oh, please, is there anybody there? '

The Secrets of Beacon Court

She was trembling and feeling faint as she stood up and stumbled to Angela's apartment, banging on the door.

After what seemed an age Angela opened it to find Bunty hardly able to blurt out, 'It's Ambrose. Oh dear God, Angela, he's on the floor in the library, he's been hurt; I think he must be dead'.

Only half awake, Angela pushed past her to the library and, kneeling beside him, saw she was right ... how had it come to this? Mind racing, shock setting in, she frantically tried to think through what to do next, knowing that there was nothing to be done but call an ambulance and the Guards. Within moments, the other residents realised another drama was unfolding in the house and popped out to investigate, while Sean Salinger was coming in from his morning run, appropriately dressed, as ever, in his stylish sports gear.

In no time the library filled up with stunned and dumbstruck neighbours…until Mitzi arrived, screaming at what she saw. She was the last to arrive, having been out partying the night before; Jimmy hadn't made it home at all!

Being one of the calmest and more clear thinking of the residents, Geraldine Haven went to Angela's side and offered to help, calling the authorities and suggesting that everybody return to their apartments until the situation was dealt with. Not that some of them paid a blind bit of notice, as ever. In any event, she locked the entrance hall door and steered Angela, Mitzi and Bunty into Mitzi's apartment.

The Secrets of Beacon Court

Poor Bunty occupied herself making sweetened tea for herself and the others for the shock, while upstairs Effie Boyle and Kitty Rae comforted each other with a little brandy, pondering their own security and weighing whether life in such a lovely location was worth the stress Even Peter Portius, a normally inexpressive man, had obviously been shaken.

**

The morning sun on the waves at Bray would revive the lowest of spirits thought Detective Inspector Ellen O'Donnell. She was delighted with her new posting to Oldchurch, a short distance up the coast. She so loved the sea and the sea air whether summer or winter and had put in the hard yards for several years in the midlands before this promotion a month earlier.

Having grown up by the sea in Mayo, she felt claustrophobic when far away from it for too long. Spring was starting to make its presence felt and, as she resolved to resume sea swimming every day, she could manage it. It was her greatest de-stressor and she missed so much while away from the coast. Even if she couldn't get to the shore, she always had the consolation of the sea view from her lovely new apartment with its large east facing windows.

A brisk walk on the promenade followed by a takeaway coffee in Catalyst was the perfect start to her day. She was due in at 10 a.m. for further 'getting to know you' and induction team meetings. So far, so good. Her new colleagues were generally welcoming and seemed unfazed to have their first female D.I. on their team.

The Secrets of Beacon Court

Her Detective Sergeant, Caroline (Carrie) King, was the longest serving member of the Oldchurch station and was a mine of information, an invaluable resource. Ellen had sensed only one slightly hesitant reaction to her at that stage, it was that of her Superintendent, Kevin Downes. Maybe she was being overly sensitive, as was quite possible, though she wondered if he had reservations about her. Still, it was early days. She would show him over time that she was more than up to the job.

The coffee from Catalyst was excellent. As she savoured the aroma, she felt set up for the day. Just as well ... her work phone was ringing as she got into the car. It was D.S. King A suspicious death had been reported nearby in an apartment complex in a mansion called Beacon Court.

Carrie was already on her way there, "See you there shortly Inspector,' she said, "you'll know the way. It is close to your own place in Old Connaught House …. what are the odds of your first serious crime investigation here being so close to home?

CHAPTER TWO

O'Donnell drove up towards the large mansion that had very recently been converted into a number of apartments in Rathmichael. The traffic was light, so she did not need to use the siren.

She turned into the elegant driveway and parked her car. She was expecting to see D.S. King's car, but she must have been delayed.

The Forensics team had just arrived and were putting on their protective suits. Making her way to the main entrance of the house, O'Donnell thought that this must be a beautiful place to live. As she entered the impressive hallway, she could see four people near the body of a man

23

lying on the floor. A woman was kneeling near it, another was comforting her. A young man in sports gear was hovering, not knowing what to do. Another, older woman, was advancing purposefully towards Ellen, who introduced herself, holding open her identification card.

"Hello Inspector," she said, 'I am Geraldine Haven and I live upstairs. I am afraid Mr Finnegan has been found dead. It has all been rather a shock. We don't really know what happened. The cleaner, Mrs. McGilligan, found him lying there on the floor." I've been trying to clear the scene, but everybody is in great distress, as you can imagine.'

At that moment, the S.C.I. team entered with all their equipment. Ellen excused herself and went to talk to Dr Gerry Donovan, the forensic specialist.

The Secrets of Beacon Court

As they walked across to the group by the body, she introduced herself and Dr Donovan. 'The doctor is a forensic specialist.' she said. He and his team will need to examine this area very carefully. I know it must have been a terrible shock, but can I ask you to return to your apartments and I will come to talk to you individually about what happened to Mr ... 'er ...Mr Finnegan ... Mr Ambrose Finnegan."

Angela and Mitzi stood up then and moved towards Angela's apartment.

The detective turned and spoke with a calm but authoritative voice. ''Please could you all return to your apartments now, and be careful not to touch anything. I will come and find you to get your statements soon. You may not leave the building until you have been interviewed and had your fingerprints taken."

Two uniformed Guards arrived at that moment and Ellen directed them to secure the scene and guard the entrance, not allowing anyone to leave or enter. They told her Detective Sergeant King would be arriving shortly. D.I. O'Donnell then went into Angela and Ambrose's apartment. It was exceptionally large, with a beautiful view of the sea, but it was in quite a mess.

There was stuff everywhere. Drawers and cupboards had been ransacked. Clearly someone was looking for something.

Ellen asked Mitzi to make some coffee while she began questioning Angela.

"Have you any idea who did this?"

Angela said "No, I have not."

"Someone was looking for something. Do you have any idea what it might have been?"

Angela shook her head again. "No."

"Where were you when this happened?"

"I was asleep in bed." Angela replied.

"And was Mr Finnegan with you?"

"Yes, he was, but we had been out and had a few drinks with friends last night, and I was tired and in need of a really deep sleep and I didn't hear a thing. I can't believe that he is, he is - dead!"

She began to cry again.

The coffee arrived at that moment and Angela took the cup and had a sip. She reached for a tissue and dried her eyes. O'Donnell let Angela have a few moments to herself. Mitzi handed her a mug of coffee and asked her if she took milk. The coffee was welcome but not as good as the earlier cup from Catalyst. Oh, for a long flat white

***

Detective Sergeant King parked her car and made her way across to the imposing entrance. She had a quick chat with the two uniformed Guards on the door and went into the house to view the scene of the crime.

The forensic team were hard at work and were bagging the book that they told her was found by the body.

The D.S. put on her disposable gloves and looked at the book through the bag. It was written in a foreign language that looked to be Chinese or Japanese. She handed it back to Dr. Donovan, "I'd like to look more closely at this later." She said, "Can you arrange that when you are done with it? And do you have any idea of the cause of death yet?"

Donovan stood up and cleared his throat. ''He was hit on the head from behind with a heavy blunt instrument. Given the blood splatter and contusion behind the left ear, I would say he died instantly, at about 5 or 6 a.m., but I will know more when I run some tests. From just looking at the body though, he has probably been dead for about three or four hours. There is some evidence of a struggle over near the bookcase and my guess is it could have something to do with the book. And you might be interested in this; we found a postcard under the body."

He handed her a plastic evidence bag with a postcard in it. The postcard had a picture of a ship on it and there was a word on the other side; but it was blurred.

"Interesting, thanks Gerry. Can you focus on this and see if you can get a clearer image of the writing? No need to say that we will need your report as soon as possible! Let me know if you find anything of interest when you get back to the lab. Do you know where I can find Inspector O'Donnell?"

"She is interviewing this man's partner in the apartment next the door."

D.S. King made her way to Angela's apartment where O'Donnell was sitting with her. After introducing them, O'Donnell continued speaking gently to Angela, "I'm so sorry for your loss. I promise you we will leave no stone unturned to find out what happened here."

Angela looked up at her, with tears streaming down her face again, and said, "I can't believe this has happened to Ambrose, why Ambrose? He was only ..." She stopped speaking and began to cry again.

Mitzi appeared at the kitchen door and suggested Angela might need some space to get dressed. Ellen told her that they would need to talk to her again as soon as she felt up to it, and she asked her to vacate the apartment then for a few hours after she was dressed, so that forensics could have a look. Angela nodded and stood up, making her way to the bedroom. Mitzi followed, shutting the bedroom door behind them. A muffled hissing sort of noise was coming from the bedroom. What were they whispering about? They looked at each other knowingly, and then left the flat and went outside to talk, exchanging their thoughts on the information gleaned so far. They also agreed an interview plan for the remaining residents of Beacon Court.

Comparing their first thoughts, O'Donnell said that she thought Angela seemed genuinely shocked and upset, but Mitzi appeared to be unmoved and strangely remote. She was also concerned that Jimmy, Mitzi's partner, had still not returned to the house. Geraldine, who had given them the names of the residents, had told them this but Mitzi had not mentioned it. Carrie said she would put out a call for Jimmy to be located and brought in for questioning, and she told Ellen about the postcard found under the body. They both agreed that the sisters knew much more than they had disclosed, and that there was more to come.

CHAPTER THREE

Opening the gate with his fob, the handsome, charming, dark-haired postman, drove down the avenue in his An Post van and was amazed at the scene in front of his eyes. Usually on his rounds the place was quiet, with residents tucked behind their apartment doors, and squinting through lace curtains or blinds, at any movement on the tarmac. Sometimes, when the sun was shining, he would salute a person strolling around or sitting reading on one of garden seats with a brisk "Good Morning." Now he could see a couple of Gardai in uniform, and two in plain clothes - obviously detectives. They were in the porch of the big house with the forensic crew, discussing the horrific incident, that had occurred a few hours ago. The residents in Beacon Court liked this enigmatic French man and wondered why he was doing such a mundane job, surmising, perhaps, there were exciting other things going on his world. He was earlier than usual that day, and Effie Boyle, who secretly fancied him, was the first person to grab hold of his arm as she ran excitedly towards him. She divulged in detail the gory details of the victim's death, murdered by a blow to the head made by a heavy object.

When she had left her grandiose life - flying or sailing to exotic places at a whim - she had retired here to live a peaceful life. Happy in her own skin, only mixing with the residents on her terms,

Effie did tend to exaggerate the incidents she encountered, no matter how trivial, to enhance her self-importance. Somehow, maneuvering around the Garda cordon, Effie dragged Lucien, for that was the postman's name, into the library; ignoring what the detective had told them about not disturbing the crime scene.

Lucien was mesmerised, not by the body on the floor, but by the purplish colour the blood had produced on the victim's elegant tailored blue suit. He observed quietly the splattered blood on the dead man's long greasy hair, vivid streaks down his neck that made his crisp white shirt a reddish colour. In his previous life, as an art student in Paris, Lucien had painted only boring exercises. Here, before him, was bizarre proof that blue and red did indeed create the colour purple. Snapping back to reality, he shuffled out of the building only to be confronted by an angry Detective Sergeant King, who promptly escorted him back to his vehicle and directed him to leave straight away.

Effie was the type of person one could not easily pigeonhole as she flitted airily through the grounds, ignoring anyone who came into her line of vision, engrossed totally in her own little world, obsessed with the invisible creatures that invade her consciousness. An only daughter, her mother had died in childbirth, after which her father, a wealthy whiskey distillery owner, left her for a dancer from the National Ballet of Ireland, abandoning her and going abroad with his lover never to return to Ireland. She, nonetheless, had great love and affection for him and had believed he would always be there for her. She was living on a trust fund he had set up for her. She never re-married after her first brief and tragic experience, but she was financially independent and free to do as she wished at any moment of the day or night. She was not fazed by authority and could not care less when the detective castigated her for bringing the young Frenchman into the crime scene and making the job of the police and forensic crew more difficult.

CHAPTER FOUR

When the detectives were informed that the crime scene was clear, the next step was to return to Beacon Court and speak with the residents, who were now witnesses.

First on D.I O'Donnell's list was Salinger. The apartment was sparsely but tastefully furnished in a mainly charcoal, black and navy palette. The only colour she noticed was the purple hyacinth in a planter, amongst flittered papers on a disorganised desk.

His apartment was in total contrast to Angela and Ambrose's which was all period décor and in keeping with the rest of the fine old house.

Salinger was of medium height, casually dressed, and in his late thirties. Whilst offering her a coffee he gestured to where he would like her to sit. He was eager to know how the investigation was progressing.

He told Ellen that this had really shaken everyone, and they were nervous now and some would be afraid to leave their apartments. O'Donnell sat opposite Salinger, explaining that their conversation was more a chat than an interview.

"How long have you lived in here?" she asked.

"He was amenable, forthcoming and generous with his information. He had

The Secrets of Beacon Court

moved to Beacon Court four years earlier, and worked as a financial trader.

Ellen said she thought he must be a pressurised and stressful job working in such an 'up and down' recession?"

Salinger's reply was slightly defensive, "A good investor will always be a good investor, I didn't get this far relying on market conditions only".

"How well did you know Ambrose?"

Salinger replied. "We both went to Stonewell College. I had lost touch with him apart from Facebook posts and then, when I bought here, and he ended up freeloading from Angela … well … yes you could say I got to know him pretty well again. Since moving in here we have seen lots of each other. Our social circles overlap … used to overlapped, rather."

O'Donnell gave Salinger a moment, then asked "What time do you leave for the office?

"Oh, in trading the hours are sporadic, so some days I work from home"

"And were you planning to do so today?'

"Yes", he replied, "I was onto Tokyo early; and took my run later than usual".

"What time did you leave?"

"I left at about 8.00, did my usual 15 kilometres and I was back at 9 o'clock"

"Did you see anything unusual when leaving for your run?" she inquired, taking notes as he explained that he always took the rear entrance so as not to disturb other residents or bring in mud from his trail run. But this morning when he was passing the front entrance on his way back from the run, he noticed Bunty, Kitty Rae and Geraldine all looking anxious and stressed in the entrance hall/library.

He was becoming upset as he spoke, ''I just cannot believe this,' he said 'I am dumbfounded. It's so awful."

O' Donnell assured him it was a natural response after such an experience …. especially when it is someone close to you.' She said, before thanking him for his time and making to leave. Walking out of the door, she told him the investigation was ongoing and that she was would be speaking to each resident individually. "If you think of anything else just let me know." And then, giving him her card, she asked. "Have any of your neighbours in Beacon Court invested with you?"

Salinger's face turned grey, but he said that he couldn't legally divulge any client details without the express permission or without a court order.

O'Donnell left, saying nothing further. But as Sean closed the door, he berated himself, why had he encouraged Ambrose to invest in a Japanese Affinity Scheme?

Why had he persuaded Geraldine to give him her Trust Funds to invest?

As for the twins' financial affairs ... what was he thinking.

CHAPTER FIVE

O'Donnell and King sat in the car outside Oldchurch Garda Station in silence. She felt like breaking into tears, her unfinished long flat white from Catalyst was by then resembling a mug of day-old porridge. She quietly questioned as to whether she had made the right career choice in moving from boring, tranquil, "nothing happens town of Tulsk" to this!! She, along with her colleague Carrie, had been unexpectedly interrogated and subsequently berated by Superintendent Kevin Downes and he was right, so bloody right. They were both mortified, ashamed, and deflated.

The previous day, thinking the Superintendent was at the Galway Races, hobnobbing in the Fianna Fail Tent with beer drinking TD's, the great and the good, and the Garda Commissioner, Ellen and Carrie had finished the day earlier than expected. It was proving difficult to round up the residents, some of whom seemed traumatized and not up to being interviewed.

They set up arrangements for the following day and, being a record sunny spring day, Ellen decided to implement her de-stress regime. Feeling brave she decided to take her first swim, minus the wet suit, in the sea at Bray, and ponder the mountain of work ahead.

Carrie had a weigh-in with the Cabinteely Weight Watchers group and, having binged on Spice of India take-outs all weekend, would have to sit in the sauna in Westwood, Leopardstown for two hours beforehand, as a damage limitation exercise.

The two detectives planned to make an early start the next morning to put together a timeline of events and leads, to finish the residents' interviews, check CCTV, and narrow down any initial suspects.

That would not happen. Ellen, after a truly short dip, had ended up cold and shivering, and needing a hot whiskey which quickly warmed her.

The subtle aroma reminded her of home and so she had a couple more, in fact many more; leaving her in awful shape the following day. King's weigh in did not go too well either. Suffering from de-hydration after a ninety-minute stint in the sauna she was faint and ill and unable to even drive herself home.

Another gym member gave her a lift home, but she had a bus journey and long walk to retrieve her car the next day. Delayed as they were this morning however, they met at 10.30 at Dunkin Do-nuts with their loyalty, 50% off, vouchers to get their box of Boston Crème and coffees to fortify them for the long day ahead.

While their order was being assembled, Carrie's mobile rang. "Morning Superintendent" she said, cheerfully forcing a smile that quickly vanished.

The Superintendent was barking down the phone. King went pale; she knew he wanted results ... and fast ... and she tried to explain, "No, not yet; we were going to put that together this morning."

Downes continued to shout at O'Donnell and King at them. "It's 24 hours since the murder and we have nothing, nothing ... nothing ... nothing! You should have had a working theory before the Crime Scene Investigators left Beacon Court.

All angles should have been covered, all leads identified and all persons of interest given their initial interview."

There was no sign of a break in, he pointed out, nothing had been robbed, so was it drugs related ... and what about motive? One of the four L's (Lust Loathing Love or Loot) Where is your timeline, your list of leads, suspects, interview notes, and your CCTV information?' There are eight residents in the house, and, in 24 hours, you have spoken to just two. What I can't get my head around, is how you haven't interviewed the cleaner; she ought to be able to give you something on the more recent 'goings on' in the house. For feck's sake King, you know the place is a bloody nuthouse. Have you even briefed O'Donnell on all the shit going on there two years ago? Knock knock knock" he roared, slapping his desk; "Good God, has that a bearing? Connect the dots woman. Two years ago, no one would come forward to backup Geraldine Haven's complaints, or even talk to us about them, have you considered what that means?"

King and O'Donnell stood in shocked silence, King's face, still glowing from the previous day's basting session in the Sauna, was now throbbing red. Neither detective wanted to open their mouth and be at the receiving end of another one of Downes's lashings, but it was too late …

he was in full tornado form. They dare hardly take a breath before he was off again.

"Bunty McGilligan knows it all you'll find" He said, "That cleaner could probably hand you over your prime suspect. Come to think of it, she would probably have the case solved by now. You two have not even talked to her, you are just pussy footing around that entitled princess and that other idiot ... a yuppie whose head is stuck up his Aston Martin DB7's rear-end."

Downes red in the face and marching up and down his office roared, even louder. "I want this case to be your absolute priority; the commissioner is on my back and I want him off it. O'Donnell, you have a day to get together your list of suspects, people you have interviewed, and all persons of interest identified. And it is to be done thoroughly. Got me? Get that tech nerd … what is his name?"

"Lucas?" said King, timidly.

"Yes him! Have him turn everyone's social media accounts upside down and inside out. Were any of them on Book-face, or that Face rubbish thing? What relationship did the two Bobbsey twins have with the world? D'you know? And what sordid world were their boyfriends in? This whole thing has stunk for years. We were warned, yet we did nothing." Said Downes, pausing a moment with his eyes dilating he was so wound up.

"I know the twins' father, the man who owns Beacon Court, Rory Carthusian. Jesus, if he knew his legacy, and the legacy of those who went before him, had come down to this – a murder and all sorts of skullduggery … well … he'd have a fit, with his magnificent ancestral home embroiled in an underground criminal world. It would make Lourdes Mansions look like … like … Fraggle Rock" he stammered. "And Rory … My God, senile he may-be," Downes went on, "but he is sharper than those entitled lazy princesses and their no-good boyfriends put together. Far sharper." He added as an after-thought, while staring sadly into the air.

Then he let fire again, "O'Donnell get the finger out. If I hear you rabbiting on about how nice it is to be beside the sea, I will personally bring you closer to it, I will even gladly throw you into it with a large block around your neck. There has not been a murder in Oldchurch in years, but there will be three in a week if you two do not get cracking. You have been handed a case on a plate that should have been solved yesterday and now we have a murderer walking free; possibly within Beacon Court's walls. Well not on my watch! And, King, I expected better than this from you; that French twat of a postman, who you call Mr "Allo Allo", has more insight into this murder which he shared with me in the 30 seconds exchange I had while he delivered the post.

All I can see here is your non-existent detective work ... take in the big picture, the house, the activity, the occupants. Christ, Kitty Rae could summon more clarity from one of those spirits she talks to at the poxy séances she holds. I'm off to find Jimmy Hennessy now ... you know what you have to do." But where was Jimmy that night? Who knew?

The Secrets of Beacon Court

Downes had a fair idea, but he wasn't for sharing it.

It had been a highly un-pleasant rant; O'Donnell had never heard anything like it before. As it happened King was more used to Downes' fiery temperament, but she had never seen him this worked up. Was it that he was pulled away early from the VIP tent in Galway? Did he lose his shirt there on the horses or at a card game, he was known to be a frequent loser at such event? What got him so worked him up about Beacon Court and all its occupants?

Her mind wandered to Downes' connections to the house. She knew Kitty Rae had tried to talk the superintendent into a séance she had intended having in her apartment earlier in the year, with her friend the floor manager from The Gate

Theatre and a few others odd balls. Carrie had laughed at the idea but, strangely, it had really spooked Downes. Kitty had told him he could talk to his deceased parents if he wanted but 'Oh Jesus,' he'd said to himself, "No way … there is no way I will do that."

King also privately suspected the Superintendent had taken investment advice from Sean Salinger.

The Superintendent did in fact know Sean Salinger, not that he would readily admit it now.

One random evening in a dingy Bray casino he met Sean at the roulette table. Not in the public area but in the private "no limits room", a sort of VIP room, not luxurious, but was less of a kip than the rest of it, and you could get a sneaky drink there once you were known and active at the table.

The Secrets of Beacon Court

That night the Superintendent was losing badly and sweating profusely, but Salinger, who was down thousands, was calm and completely undeterred. Wearing a Louis Copeland suit and a Cartier watch he looked young and dapper a far cry from Downes red face and his beer belly pulling his shirt buttons apart to afflict the sight of any unfortunate observers. They had a couple of brandies together. When Sean offered the Superintendent a lift home Downes initially declined, but then he saw Salinger climb into his Aston Martin DB7 Vantage.

"Christ" he thought, "I've only seen one of those, and that was on the television.

The temptation was too great; he could not resist the lift and the lure of the exotic life the young man seemed to have.

He had to find out how the young pup had become so wealthy and then to emulate him; Sean was making a success out of his life ... and Downes wanted a bit of it.

Over the years Kevin Downes had stayed on in the force, locked in by the prospect of an early retirement with a good pension ... but he had resented it. He'd watched several of his fellow Garda colleagues throw in the "beat work" early only to set up bars, nightclubs and even hotels. All the Guards knew there was a shortage of liquor licenses in Dublin and you could, if you were smart and had a bit of luck and foresight, transfer a rural license from a small loss-making bar into a large premise in Dublin City Centre. Executed right, you could clean up. The most famous of all was Ali Baba, owned by an ex-Garda, and the envy of them all. All the Gardai attended the place several nights a week ''on the pull'' and marveled at how the owner, ex Garda Joe Mahon, made it look so damned easy.

It was the same conversation that was had by the same gardai night after night over the same stale beer at 4.00 in the morning:

"Twenty-five grand a week on the cloakroom alone" they would mutter.

"That's nothing they take in eighty grand a week on the door admission, and that's before they sell a drink".

"Yep, all cash." Said another.

"And no money spent on Security of course!"

"Sure, aren't we all here."

"Jesus, I hear the condom machine in the toilets has the highest sales of condoms in the damned country "

"Must be the one in the Ladies toilets so...." The first man said, and they all roared laughing.

Downes had heard it a hundred times before, 'work nights out', Christmas parties.... Idiots,' he thought to himself; secretly seething that he let so many opportunities pass him by. Now with an ex-wife and two grown children it would never happen, and he knew it. The bitterness seeped from him sometimes and his colleagues bore the brunt of it.

Salinger though, by investing carefully, could be on his way to fast money and, as investing in shares was something Downes reckoned he could do, he had frequently and discretely visited Sean Salinger in Beacon Court.

The previous year he'd been a few times, looking for the inside track. He had his own share account with Blennerhasset and Hunt and, following a tip from Salinger, he was soon investing his inheritance from his parents into Lehman Brothers, the fourth largest investment bank in the States. Unknown to both of them, it would come a cropper within a year but not before Sean and Kevin had become heavily invested.

Even at the point when the bank was heading for a near 50% loss, Sean counseled Downes; 'It's the market over-reacting.' He told him, hoping to give him some reassurance. "It's too big to fail, take advantage …. You'll never get in again at these low prices again; buy more." And Downes, to his cost, did. Salinger was in the worst position at the worst time and did not know it. He was young enough to expect that markets bounce back, but not old enough to experience a total market collapse.

That lack of experience would cost him a lot personally, but even worse was his exposure in managing the accounts of the twins and their boyfriends. Acting for some of the other residents of Beacon Court as well, and circumventing anti-money laundering regulations, he had invested some large deposits of what he assumed was mostly family money. But family money it was not; unknown to him at the time, in the case of the twins, the money had passed through the hands of some of the worst criminals in the country. Sean Salinger's recklessness had cost a lot of people a lot of money … and Downes, although reckless himself, was one who would not forget it … ever!

***

The Secrets of Beacon Court

Outside Oldchurch Station, O'Donnell and King looked at each other in desperation. They would need to act fast and get results. They needed to finish interviewing the other occupants of Beacon Court who were now somewhat either nervous or elusive.

Most important, however was to talk to Bunty McGilligan, the cleaner, and away from the house at that.

O'Donnell drove them to Bunty's place while King brought her up to date about other events that had rattled the occupants of Beacon Court. King explained that frequent anonymous calls had been received at the station concerning disturbances in the house, possibly normal domestic arguments but no one was prepared to give their names and the few details they got were vague and hard to act on.

One night a call to the Guards was made by Kitty Rae. She suspected a break-in was about to happen, that there was someone lurking suspiciously outside.

But when the Gardai arrived they found her so inebriated with brandy they couldn't make any sense of what she was saying and the next day, when they asked her again, she had no idea she had even made the call.

Another time, King recalled, there had been a commotion early in the morning after an alleged twelve-hour party, and when the twins woke up the next day, each was in bed with the other one's boyfriend. The Garda taking their statements got them mixed up too he was so confused, and everything in his report then had to be nullified or struck out.

"We had Geraldine Haven drop into the Oldchurch station twice about two years ago." King said, "She wanted to lodge a complaint, or see if we could investigate some strange late-night activity around the garden. In her "line of work at the Justice Department", she said, she was all too familiar with criminal gangs and their brutal modus operandi.

Maybe she was overly anxious when she'd witnessed the high powered and expensive 4X4's arriving in late at night, a number of them with Northern Irish registrations. Their lights were always switched off as they entered and exited, and she thought some heavy bags had been exchanged; elements, she believed, of a sinister criminal gang.

But nothing of substance happened again, and she would not put her name to anything she had told us about, so we had nothing to go on. We called another day, following up on other issues and they were all outside having afternoon tea … laughing and joking and no signs of anything sinister or suspicious".

O'Donnell glanced across at King, as she recounted what an unusual and contradictory place Beacon Court was, and how odd were the people who lived there.

It was going to be a long day.

CHAPTER SIX

Bunty McGilligan heard a car pull into the drive of her small cottage in Ashford. She sat there for a moment, thinking as she took a long drag of her silk cut purple. She knew it was the Gardai and she knew why they were there.

Lots of things had gone through Bunty's mind since the previous day's calamity. On her drive home in her little Toyota Yaris, she had mulled over her previous life. The life no one knew she lived. A chartered accountant working and making vast sums of money for a Saudi rare book dealer, Bunty knew how and where you can hide money. She had learned a lot in Saudi Arabia, specifically how lucky she was to get back to Ireland just before she may have been heading for a sweaty filthy Saudi prison.

Bunty also knew the residents of Beacon Court pitied her, and she wanted it that way. They had no idea who she really was, and she would never tell them. She reminisced about the life she had lived, the wealth she had seen and experienced, and how things might have been. If only ..!

Now, each day, she drove home to a drunk hopeless 'live-in lover' Benny and a faithful dog who was truly the only object of affection she had left. When Bunty thought of Benny, her emotions shifted to wondering 'why he cannot just keel over and die.' The house, the pokey little cramped cottage in Ashford was the only thing keeping her in the relationship. While tiny, the site itself was valuable and, one day, he will be gone. Then, maybe, peace! As soon as the thought of peace surfaced, she felt a shiver run up her spine. Peace was a rare feeling for Bunty; her past would always loiter in her mind and continue to haunt her every dream.

That afternoon, as she stubbed her cigarette in the ashtray and got up to answer the door to the waiting detectives, she smiled to herself. She knew one thing for sure - she was the clever one around there. Whoever she wanted to go down for murder, she could make it happen. She would play with them first though, she reflected to herself.

She glanced at Benny, frying sausages, and felt her stomach lurch. What else have I got to do today she thought! I may as well become just good old "Bunty the cleaner".

She opened the door to the two gardai: O'Donnell and King. "Hello dears", she said, while silently observing that O'Donnell walked like a culchie and King, my God, she *has* put on the pounds. She invited the detectives into the front room, a very small, cold, dark room. There was a fireplace with months' old ashes and a stench of stale cigarettes. The room was filled with books. Something both detectives noticed immediately. They were not Mills and Boon either, they were on art, history, culture, and travel.

"Nice lot of books you have, Bunty", King commented. "Who is the avid reader"?

"It's Benny, well … he used to read a lot when he was sober but he's not doing much of it anymore. I keep meaning to donate them to a bookshop."

O'Donnell wondered what book seller would want be desperate to take them; they were covered in dust and stained yellow from cigarette smoke. She then explained that they wanted to speak to Bunty about what had occurred in Beacon Court on the previous day. Bunty offered the two detectives tea but they both declined, wanting to get out of there as quicky as possible.

Bunty then went through the previous mornings' events for them.

She had arrived just before 9 a.m. and was about to start her usual morning routine. "When I first saw him, I thought he'd just passed out from drink; it's a sight

71

I've seen before. And I was about to start cleaning around him," she said, "when I noticed his colour, and the blood coming from his head. That's when I ran screaming."

She hesitated a moment after that, and then went on to tell them she had a bad heart and her hands were inclined to shake. She watched their impatience as they tried to mask it with false empathy. She was enjoying every minute of playing "Bunty the cleaner".

King asked if there was anything else besides her trauma she would like to add to her statement. But Bunty shook her head and then, after a pause O'Donnell thought was going to last forever, she said: "No, I don't think there is … though I did hear the twins whispering about money one day. It was probably nothing; they were talking about rare books. *Now* I believe they might have been talking about cleaning them, as I heard something about 'laundering' - a word that surprised me … neither of them have even *seen* a washing machine let alone used one."

"When do you reckon this was?"

"About a month ago."

"O'Donnell nodded, thoughtfully. And then she and King went over the notes they had taken; warning Bunty that they may need to speak to her again.

"Of course, ladies, anytime" she replied, confidently.

O'Donnell and King got up to leave then, and Bunty showed them to the door; waving them off, while gently grinning to herself.

After they had gone, she went to her bedroom at the back of the cottage, sat at her dressing table and opened the second drawer from the top.

From it she took out the bible, with its beautiful, embellished gold font, and then she opened it.

Yes! She thought, taking off the outer cover and revealing the treasure that lay beneath … an original copy of the amazing and priceless 'Rothchild Prayerbook'.

Reaching forward she took it in her hands; gently stroked for a few seconds, and then put it back before hurrying out to the kitchen to fill Benny's glass. 'The sooner I've got you sorted the better,' she thought.

CHAPTER SEVEN

Although still in deep shock, once they heard the front door close and saw the detectives' cars leave the grounds, Angela sat Mitzi down and told her they had to talk, urgently. The forensics team were still in the hall and dusting the apartment down for prints to compare. They would have to come up with a plan … and quickly. Fortunately, neither was the witless party girl they had led the world to believe.

Angela sat in her flat with Mitzi, reflecting on their lives. When they had first shacked up with Ambrose and Jimmy, they were the ones pulling the strings on a global drugs cartel. Before his ''dementia'' their father, Rory, had brought them up in a glamorous world of global travel, and they were used to the high life. They had contacts all over the world, Dubai, South Africa and the States, but things had got out of hand over the previous couple of months. Jimmy was not happy, he felt that he and Ambrose were just puppets, and they were trying to take over from Angela and Mitzi, which in turn led to big fights and wild reconciliation parties. Angela, fed up with Ambrose trying to be the boss, had started a casual relationship with Sean Salinger. It was convenient; when Ambrose was out with his mates or even if they were out together, Ambrose always drank too much and often stayed out all night. She would grab a taxi home and spend the night with Sean. That is why she could not understand Sean's account of his movements earlier that morning, and she wondered if the police would pick up on it.

Angela thought back over the last few hours or so. She had been with Sean the previous night. He was working from home, as he said, and he did go out for a run, but the strange thing was … to get to the back entrance he had to pass through the hall, which meant he should have seen Ambrose lying there! Why wasn't the alarm raised sooner? She needed to check with Mitzi as to what she saw when she came home in the early hours.

As Angela had left Sean's apartment earlier, she had had to pop into the lift to avoid the staircase she generally used to get back without being seen. Not that her relationship with Sean was much of a secret anymore, she thought, with all the prying eyes in the place.

She had just arrived back in the ransacked apartment when Bunty came hammering at the door.

Angela and Mitzi were not totally surprised to hear about what had happened to Ambrose as he really had been mixing with the wrong people; trying to make contacts and connections to take over their business. It was only likely to be a matter of time before she was going to dump him, but it was convenient to have a man around who people thought was in charge. The twins decided they would try to continue as they did normally once they found out where Jimmy was. Mitzi tried to remember where exactly they had been that night, and who they were with. She finally spoke to an old friend of Jimmy's who told her they had shared a taxi together and that he had hopped out at the gate and the last he saw of him, he was stumbling up the avenue singing 'New York, New York'! So, if he had made it that far where was he now?

***

Peter Portius was curious. He had been watching the goings on in Beacon Court with great interest. He let it be known that he was a retired customs officer from South Africa, but he was actually an Interpol agent, now tasked with gathering information on drugs and 'people trafficking' cartels which had been operating in Dublin, and southern Ireland going back many generations. They had been investigating this activity for years, when Portius got an odd sounding email from a distant relative telling him about some strange happenings at Beacon Court.

They had started corresponding when Portius was doing some research on his Irish ancestors. This distant cousin lived in nearby Old Connaught House, who learning of Portius's successful career in Interpol, thought he might be interested in some local mysterious activities.

The cousin's best friend, Geraldine Haven, happened to be a resident in Beacon Court, and was quite disturbed and frightened on occasions, by what she thought were sinister transactions occurring late at night at the house. This friend had a lifetime of experience working in the Department of Justice so she reckoned she knew what she was talking about! Peter knew from the correspondence with Geraldine, and earlier intelligence, that this was no ordinary scenario and, without saying anything to his newly found cousin, he arranged with Interpol to go undercover as a retired customs officer from South Africa. From what he observed, he was quite surprised at the sloppy way the local police were dealing with the current situation, and the distinctly lethargic way they were going about their business. Whilst he had been living there, he had discovered quite a lot about the residents of the house and none of them was beyond suspicion. The police really did need to conduct an immediate search of the grounds to try and find the murder weapon, and to check the whereabouts of everyone over the previous two or three days.

After the morning they had had with Downes, D.I. O'Donnell and D.S. King were determined to get their act together. They had dropped the ball and were feeling the consequences and, in the car on the way back from questioning Bunty McGilligan, they confirmed that the forensic team was back in Beacon Court searching for the murder weapon. They'd finish with the witnesses first, starting with Mitzi, as she and Angela had obviously been discussing something quite urgent when they left the day before.

King knocked on Mitzi's door and she let them in, invited them to sit down, and asked if they would like a coffee. They both said no and sat with their notebooks at the ready. They needed to know where she was the night before the murder; where she'd been; who she'd been with and … if there'd been any sign of Jimmy.

She had barely opened her mouth to say 'No' when O'Donnell's phone pinged. She had a quick look. It was from the forensics team, asking her to step outside into the grounds as soon as possible.

She glanced over to Carrie King and said she needed to 'pop out for five minutes' and that she would leave the interview to her. When Carrie nodded, she left the apartment, crossed the hall, and went outside where she could see the line of forensic searchers gathered in the fringe of the woods.

They had come to stand-still and Dr Donovan was waving to her. 'Come on;' he shouted, 'we've found another body."

CHAPTER EIGHT

Ellen hurried across the car park and down to the wood where Dr. Donovan was waiting, He told her a man's body had been found in the undergrowth and that an area around it had been cordoned off and polystyrene blocks laid down so they could access it without disturbing any of the evidence.

What was particularly interesting though, was that this body seemed to have the same injuries as the one in the hall at the main house.

'I'll be able to give you more information on time of death and probable cause when I get him back to the morgue.'

The Secrets of Beacon Court

Donovan said; which prompted O'Donnell to ask if he could at least give her an estimate of the time of death.

Donovan laughed; he never liked being asked for rushed estimates but knew she'd only keep on asking, so he told her that, 'taking into consideration the lividity of the body, he's probably been dead about 30 hours.'

At that moment the coroner's officers arrived to remove the corpse and, as they put it into the body bag, they saw he'd been lying on something underneath.

On closer examination, it was another book, a hardback with a very ornate cover, again in a foreign language either Chinese or Japanese. Ellen asked the forensic team to bag up the new evidence and take it back to the station and, when they'd gone, Dr Donovan showed her a bloodstained bookend with fragments of bone and hair and what looked like brain-matter, caught on one of the edges. 'It was a couple of feet away from the body.' He said. Don't quote me on this just yet, Inspector, but it looks to me as though it might be the murder weapon used on both victims,"

Before the coroner's van took the second corpse away Donovan checked the dead man's clothing, finding a wallet in the pocket of the trousers.

Ellen donned a pair of forensic gloves and carefully opened up the wallet. Inside was just over 800 euro in cash and two cheques made out for 1,000 euro each, made payable to J. Hennessy. One of the cheques was signed by E. Boyle and the other by G. Haven. Ellen couldn't help wondering why these two ladies were making out cheques for large amounts of money to one of their neighbours.

"The victim's going to turn out to be Jimmy Hennessy, I think." Said Ellen to Dr Donovan ... "the man who never returned home. I'll go back up to the house and see if we can get someone to positively identify him before the coroner's men take him."

By the time she'd got back to the house she'd decided Sean Salinger was going to be the best option; she didn't want Mitzi unnecessarily called to identify someone who may not be her missing boyfriend so she ran lightly up the stairs to the first floor and knocked on Sean's door.

When she couldn't hear anything inside, she called out to him that it was the

Guards and that they needed his assistance with a delicate matter.

Then she heard someone approaching the door and, as it slowly opened, Sean Salinger gingerly peered out, "How can I help you Inspector?" he said.

"I'm afraid I need you to come downstairs with me." O'Donnell replied, "We have found a body in the woods which we believe may be Jimmy Hennessy and we'd appreciate it greatly if you can assist us in making an identification."

"Oh my God, I've never seen a dead body until saw Ambrose's yesterday. Do I have to do it?" stuttered Sean.

"Well, no, we can't make you, but it would be really helpful to us if you wouldn't mind. Of course, we could always ask Ms. Mitzi Carthusian ... but she is already consoling her sister over her loss, and … well … we thought it would easier if you made the identification."

"When you say it like that," Sean replied, "obviously, I will help if I can, so let's get it over and done with." They went back down the stairs and out to the car park. The coroner unzipped the bag and Sean peered in,

"Jesus Christ, it's Jimmy all right, what happened to him?"

"I'm afraid we can't say at the moment" replied Ellen, "if you could keep this to yourself until I've had a chance to inform Ms. Carthusian of her boyfriend's demise, I'd be very grateful."

Just then they heard another loud shout coming up from the woods ''

Find!' All the gardai who were still searching stopped what they were doing, and Ellen ran back down to the trees. And there, in the undergrowth, and a couple of metres from where the body had been found, was a wooden chest ... and it looked as though someone had tried to bury it in the ground.

And all the time ... the rest of the Gardai who were still searching the woods ... and those who were in the car park with the undertaker, were all being carefully watched from a small window on the first floor of the house by someone who remained in the shadows as she pondered on her next move ......

HAPTER NINE

B loody idiots!" Peter Portius muttered to himself, as he watched what he called "the Keystone Cops" emerging from the scene of the finds. He couldn't imagine how they'd earned their stripes. "It wasn't due to their good looks!" he said to Lucien, the postman, when they went for one of their long walks by the sea.

Peter had grown up in Qunu, Eastern Cape, a rural area, and he had entered the Police Force aged nineteen. In 1954, a year before he was born, Peter's father, Johaan, was given the job as Estate Manager of a vast tobacco plantation in South Africa belonging to a titled man, a

Baron, whose title hailed from Old Connaught House. On his mother's side, Peter's heritage was Irish, and he identified most closely with this side, people whose history of rebellion and resistance fascinated him.

When Peter joined the police, he had no idea what he was letting himself in for, but he acquired an extraordinary knowledge of the law and had a kind manner. By the age of thirty, he had been promoted to Regional Deputy, specialising in Internal affairs. He was a cop's cop, but at the same time, a cop to watch over cops. In 1982 he was moved to Cape Town to join the fight in the battle against corruption. And in 1990, he was one of the policemen who escorted Nelson Mandela, out of prison on Robin Island. Some years after that historic event, he received an offer from Interpol to become an agent, and the beauty of the appointment was the option to choose from a range of ongoing investigations in different locations across the world. The international human trafficking trade was a cause close to him, and in recent years he had opted for an ongoing investigation in Ireland, attracted by the opportunity to reconnect with his Irish heritage.

In the early 2000s, some years after being transferred to Ireland, he came across an article in the Irish Times Online about a young couple moving into an apartment in the newly refurbished Old Connaught House and he immediately, saw his retirement 'forever home'. What an opportunity! But when he called there all the Old Connaught apartments had been sold, so he decided to rent one just up the hill at Beacon Court while waiting for an apartment to become available in Old Connaught House. Little did he know then that he was stepping straight into the hub of the very criminality he was there to investigate.

In the course of his research into his family, he had learned something of the local history of the age-old practices of slavery, or human trafficking, how it had survived and that this form of smuggling was now entangled with the international drugs trade.

Back in the 1700's, when the slave trade needed ships to carry their cargo, the Carthusians never had a shortage of sea going vessels and currently, as he was finding out, their vessels still often seemed to be to carrying sinister cargoes.

Incidentally, Portius had also learned that, during the Great Famine, the owners of Old Connaught House, ancestors of his father's employer, had doubled the wages of their farm staff while the Lady of the house had visited the poor in Little Bray and taken food from the farm to them.

The family, he discovered, had always been 'kind to the natives' but he wondered how much of their generosity was genuine and how much of it was fueled by a clever, if self-serving, strategy. In any event, Old Connaught House had survived the IRA's burning of British manor houses. The current modern Carthusian Empire had moved with the times, finding more contemporary opportunities for profiteering from trafficking; investing in Ferry companies and even airlines to provide legitimate cover. Most of the narcotics side of the business was eventually sold on and taken over by two warring Dublin gangs. The Carthusians experience in hiding and laundering the profit from these crimes, however, continued to be invaluable to these gangs. The criminal bosses involved were not overly bothered that a few of the local Gardai were actually doing quite well at interrupting, delivery and arresting minor kingpins for they were only taking the tip of a multi-billion international trade.

Though initially not connected to his Interpol assignment, in recent times Peter had become concerned by the strange behavior of some of his co-residents in Beacon Court, and he was soon wondering if any of them were, even remotely, involved in the drug smuggling and fine art forgery he was investigating. He found himself getting tit bits of information regarding the Carthusians that he didn't like, and he was beginning to wonder if he had done the right thing in moving to Beacon Court in the first place.

Bound up in these thoughts, he got quite a shock when Mitzi's scream broke the silence. She had obviously just been told of the second tragedy.

CHAPTER TEN

Mitzi was trembling from head to toe, and Angela was doing her best to comfort her, despite her own recent traumatic events. Ellen was once again struck by how similar the twins were, almost a mirrorlike reflection of each other.

It was hard to believe two sisters could each lose their partner to murder, let alone for both killings to occur on the same night. The circumstances of both deaths appeared similar, and they were working on the assumption that both men had been killed by the same weapon, which logically led to the belief that it was also the same killer they were now trying to hunt down.

The Secrets of Beacon Court

Forensics had removed the wooden chest and, once they had it back at the lab, they would be able to take it apart. Perhaps other hidden contents would reveal further clues. The blood covered bookend had also been taken to the lab, and the hope was that there would be some fingerprint evidence. They needed something of significance now to kick the case up a gear. Ellen needed to sit down and go over the facts with Carrie and compare their interview notes. There was so much to consider, so many conflicting stories they had to piece together.

They left Beacon Court via the front entrance and planned to head back to the station to compare notes. Carrie had already asked Lucas, the tech guy, to see what was on the CCTV footage from the around the premises at the times of the murders. However, as they were driving out, her mobile pinged; it was a message from him saying cameras were just for show and never actually recorded anything.

Another dead end.

As they drove away, deflated, they looked back at the Beacon Court, and were disconcerted to see so many faces watching from the windows of the building. Mitzi and Angela, still huddled together by the window in Mitzi's flat. Effie, Kitty and Geraldine looking down on them from Kitty's flat and, on the other side, there was Sean ... watching them drive away ... hands on his hips. "Was it one of you lot?" Ellen wondered, as they made their way back to the station

.

The Secrets of Beacon Court

Peter Portius was not watching the departing police. He was on Bray sea front with Lucien, the post man (having made hurried contact with him when the news of Jimmy emerged). They were in a heated discussion.

"I'm pretty sure we're getting close, Lucien, very close," Peter was saying, the wind buffeting his hair as they walked along the coast towards Bray Head.

"Yes, I agree, but there's still a lot we don't know."

Lucien, as most of the residents suspected, was much more than a post man. He'd been undercover for almost two years by then, trying to uncover dirty drug money that was getting into France from Ireland, via several routes, under the guise of rare book sales. They knew from contacts in Dubai and Saudi that the original source was Ireland, and so his bosses at Europol had sent him over to see if he could find out more. He was a brains man, not an action man, so he had been quite shocked to see the body of Ambrose Finnegan, bleeding out on the carpet of the library at Beacon Court. He and Peter had accidentally discovered they had interests in common, having at one time suspected each other. Once they knew they had the same goal, they would meet for walks during which they would fill each other in regarding new evidence they had uncovered.

Lucien was able to keep them both up to date with news from the Garda station, as he had established a good rapport with Superintendent Downes, who loved to talk. Peter also knew Downes fairly well. After a late night, rather drunken chat, in a pub, he had uncovered the fact that Downes had 'something' on Sean Salinger, and that there was no love lost between them. The two had 'bumped into' each other in Bray (Portius had actually engineered it) and Downes had wanted the lowdown on Sean when he discovered that Peter lived in the same house. He was a useful source of information, even if he didn't realize it.

Peter and Lucien suspected all was not right in the station house in Oldchurch, so didn't take the gardai based there into their confidence. They were hoping the new D.I. - Ellen O'Donnell - would be someone they could trust and confide in. They needed local help and, having jointly decided that D.S. Carrie King, as the longest serving officer in Oldchurch, was the most likely one to give it to them, they were waiting for the most appropriate moment to approach her.

Both Lucien and Peter, in the meantime, had quickly worked out that the twins had taken over the drug cartel from their father. Rory had lost control after the Irish drug lords he had been dealing with had found out that he was trying to deal forged copies of certain books and keeping the originals for his private collection. As a warning to him to toe the line, they ordered his wife to be killed in the so called "accident" in Bray. Following it, Rory had suffered a major breakdown. He lost his mind and handed the family business on to the twins before retiring to a nursing home, having paid through the nose for a diagnosis of "early on set dementia" from a dodgy doctor. He was still a quivering wreck, terrified of his own shadow, his

The Secrets of Beacon Court

incredible private collection scattered to the four winds to fund his stay in his luxurious retirement.

The girls, having no idea who they were dealing with at first, had lost control of themselves when they got hold of the purse strings, going wild with parties and drink, and there had been some close shaves with the underworld bosses, who wanted them to lower their profiles and not blow the secret activities that had been working for years. They made threats against the twins and their partners and had even driven out to the house late at night to warn them all to rein it back. That had woken the twins and their boyfriends up to the fact that millions of euro were involved here, and they needed to grow up and deal with it.

Peter and Lucien had felt that they were almost ready to present their suspicions to their bosses in Europe and beyond, but there were just a few things they needed to be clarified first. Peter had managed to get Ambrose on side; he had discovered that Angela was having an affair with Sean and, when Peter told Ambrose about it, he was furious. He didn't want to leave her though, not because he loved her, but because he was still lining himself up to take over, with Jimmy as his partner, and push the twins off their throne.

Peter convinced him that he would be better served coming over from the dark side. They could protect him if he'd give evidence against the twins, and if he told them who else in Beacon Court was involved.

The Secrets of Beacon Court

He could give Ambrose a new identity, start a new life anywhere he liked, probably anywhere in the world, as this was going to be such a big case.

Ambrose had gone as far as to confirm that Sean Salinger had been laundering money for them, the cartel, and that it was all done through the sale of rare books. He didn't really understand that side of things himself. He also revealed that there were others in the house who were involved. But then he got spooked, and said he needed time to think. He said he'd let Peter know as soon as he had made up his mind, but he was afraid of what might happen if anyone found out what was going on. Peter had given Ambrose a postcard with a house name on it. The house was in Waterford; it was a safe house managed by Lucien and his team from Europol. He told Ambrose that when he was ready, he could go to that house and he would be protected.

All he had to do was show them the card when he got there. Peter and Lucien had been ready to go, ready to whisk Ambrose to safety as soon as he agreed, but then it had all gone wrong. Ambrose had been murdered - and they prayed that he hadn't told anyone about them and blown their cover.

Now they were trying to decide if it was time to confide in D.I. O'Donnell and D.S. King. They could feel suspicious eyes being cast in their direction, and they needed to clear the way for the real suspect to be brought to justice, before the whole thing was blown wide open. Back in the

The Secrets of Beacon Court

station in Oldchurch, fresh coffees in their hands, Ellen and Carrie went over their interview notes and tried to piece together the timelines of the murders.

"You know what, Carrie?" Ellen said, "I don't trust a single bloody one of them. They all seem to be hiding something, and the timelines don't quite match up."

"I agree." said Carrie. "And what about that cleaner, Bunty, she's suspicious too. Question is, who do we bring in first?"

The phone on Ellen's desk rang; she scooped it up and listened to the voice at the other end. "Yes, right O.K. Really? Hmm, very interesting. Thanks for that." She said, hanging up the phone and looking over to Carrie. "That was forensics. We have the murder weapon - the bookend - and it does appear to have evidence of both victims' blood on it. They have deciphered the word on the back of the post card too. Best of all though,' she said, punching the air with her fist, 'they have opened the chest and you'll never believe what's in it. We have to get down there, now … right now!"

CHAPTER ELEVEN

The beautifully crafted wooden chest contained some very old looking books, a substantial amount of cash and a USB stick.

It emerged after technical analysis that the stick contained statements from Jimmy and Ambrose, downloads from Angela and Mitzi's computers, details of rare books, forgeries and originals used in a money laundering operation, as well as a fund transfer system operated by Salinger. These records were the boys' passports out of this murky world, as well as immunity from prosecution and protection from the wrath of the gangs. They would make a new start, maybe even somewhere warm and exotic!

Ambrose had persuaded Jimmy to join him in his plan to expose the operation and become a protected witness.

Lucien had come on board, as having Jimmy's testimony strengthened the prosecution.

Reluctantly at first, Jimmy had come to see that, sooner or later, the enterprise would implode. Apart from Interpol and Europol's scrutiny, there were beginning to be cracks in the system with Salinger looking increasingly nervous and the twins pushing back on the boys' plans.

The wooden chest, custom made in the previous century for the transport of valuable books, had come from the library. The boys had managed to squirrel away a few books themselves as a little something extra for their journey. They had a couple of forgeries of oriental masterpieces still to go, hidden away in the library. All they needed to do now was set up their getaway in a way that wouldn't arouse suspicion until they were under Lucien and Peter's protection in the safe house.

**

Geraldine Haven, a pillar of the establishment, was immensely proud of her standing as a respected public servant, a key figure in the State Solicitor's office for many years. After these horrific and shocking murders, she was in dreadful state of terror and panic...not that you would know it to look at her. Years of having to have a cool head and calm demeanor stood to her now but she struggled to maintain that rationality as this awful scenario unfolded.

How was she going to manage this one! It was never meant to turn out like this. What had she unleashed and how would she survive it? She should have known of course that the truth would ultimately come out and deep down she had dreaded the day, but in her wildest dreams – or nightmares, she could never have predicted what had just happened. She was about to be ruined, reputation destroyed, and quite possibly end her days in prison…and she knew the women's prison very well from the time she served on the Visiting Committee.

What a tangled web we weave…Geraldine had long experience of covering tracks, her own and those of others. Many years ago, there had been suspicions in the Department of Justice that someone was impeding the prosecutions of certain gang related crimes. It seemed that someone was tampering with evidence, leaking information, and releasing witness names. If true, it was very artfully done, but no one was ever found by the investigating team, which included one Ms.G. Haven. The whole rotten story had started with one moment of weakness when she destroyed evidence which could have linked her brother to membership of the IRA and involvement in the kidnap and murder of a British judge. She felt she had no choice; it would have killed her parents, not to talk of it ending her career advancement. After that, it became known to certain republican leaning criminals that there was a weak link in the Department. Over the years she had had to cover her traces by providing more 'intelligence' and although she was well rewarded and built an extremely comfortable 'nest egg' from it, she was on a treadmill she could not stop. Retirement had brought some relief but then of course she had become involved with Salinger's scam, however unknowingly at first. She had handed him her lump sum plus some of her 'nest egg' to invest for her. Impressed by his obvious success, and the fact that many of the other residents in Beacon Court trusted him, she found out too late that he was operating a Madoff style 'Ponzi scheme' and that his blatant success was built on sand, it was an illusion.

Some months ago now, Geraldine had begun to wonder about Salinger's investment company. It may have been rumblings in the newspapers and on television about the global financial markets, or her friend in Old Connaught House worrying about her pension fund, but she began to feel uneasy.

When she met with Salinger to discuss her concerns, Geraldine was unconvinced by his nonchalant attitude. She did some further research which worried her and when she insisted that Sean provide documentary proof of the safety of her investment, he eventually caved in.

He confessed that he had made heavy losses on a risky but potentially lucrative investments. He had been covering his losses with income from laundering the proceeds of crime. Geraldine couldn't believe what she was hearing and even more shocking, if that were possible, was that this money was being funneled through the Carthusian twins. Apparently, the family had been involved in the money laundering business for decades. It had something to do with buying and selling rare books and involved complicated dealings substituting forgeries for originals, but he didn't have much of a grasp of the logistics of it all.

This was almost too much to take in and to process. Geraldine couldn't risk going to the authorities for fear of having to account for her own unlikely wealth, never mind cross the gangs whose ruthlessness was well known to her. The sinister goings on in the house now made sense; the strange cars and people coming and going in the night, odd snippets of arguments she had overheard between the twins and their boyfriends, Salinger's evasiveness and air of nervous tension. Even though she had lost a fortune, her main concern now shifted to her very freedom and physical safety. She thought back over the last long and dreary decades of pretense and fear of discovery. It had to end. Geraldine's brother's escapades had dogged her family for years until he 'relocated' to parts unknown. The irony was that she may now have to consider the same course of action herself! Such a disruption was the last thing she wanted to contemplate at this stage of her life but what alternative was there?

Her retirement holiday in the Maldives had planted the seed of a plan B and now it looked like becoming an urgent move. Having checked, she knew that there was no extradition treaty between Ireland and the Maldives.

Her financial situation was far less healthy than before she had stupidly handed half of it over to that conman Salinger, but it would do. Her needs were few. She would be able to access her substantial public service pension electronically from abroad, provided her secrets remained safe. She would have to see what she could recover from Salinger, if anything, and start planning her own 'relocation'. She would try to shame him into recompensing her, but she wasn't in a position to threaten him with exposure.

Pity she had given Jimmy Hennessy that cheque for the monthly rent. He had seemed particularly pressed for it this time, doing the rounds of the residents. It would have covered her air fare!

Meanwhile she would have to keep a very close watch on the 'gang of four'. In recent weeks, Jimmy and Ambrose had taken to relaxing over a drink in the library.

Geraldine had wondered at this as they didn't strike her as readers, but she assumed that they were seeking space from the twins. She often observed their meetings as she had hardly been able to sleep since Salinger's revelations.

A couple of evenings ago she was riveted when, eavesdropping, she heard them planning to drop the twins and enter an international witness protection programme. Ambrose was persuading Jimmy that it was the only course of action open to them and that he had gathered sufficient evidence for the authorities to take down the whole operation. Jimmy seemed convinced. In any event, there was really no alternative.

Geraldine was stunned. That was the end of a clean getaway for her. The evidence against the twins would lead to Salinger and ultimately implicate Geraldine, revealing her unexplained wealth. Salinger would turn over anything he had to mitigate his own situation. That would be the end of her pension and the end of her reputation. Her remaining assets would be frozen and she could wind up penniless. Jimmy and Ambrose had to be stopped. She would have to find their evidence, without which they were useless as witnesses.

Clearly time was running out. Geraldine would have to act. With great misgivings, she concluded that her only option was to re-establish a connection with her underworld contacts from some years ago. She certainly wasn't capable of taking care of things herself. She arranged that, for a substantial amount of cash, one of the gang's footsoldiers, would 'break in' and search Ambrose's apartment for whatever he could find. Ambrose must surely have a safe and a computer in the home office which he used for his so-called role managing the complex. On the night of the murders, she saw that Angela, Mitzi and the 'lads' left together for the evening and as they routinely stayed out until the early hours, she contacted her burglar and left the front door ajar.

Unbeknown to her of course, Ambrose and Jimmy had chosen that night to make their getaway. Their plan was to leave the club separately and meet outside the house, pick up the wooden chest and head down to Waterford to the safe house. Ambrose had a card with the name of the house, their destination, on it. Ambrose would pick up the few belongings they had packed, and Jimmy would dig up the chest which was shallowly covered in the wooded area near the gate. All going well, no one would miss them for a while. There was nothing new about them going awol from time to time.

***

The double tragedy unfolded when Ambrose surprised the 'burglar 'in the middle of ransacking his apartment. Ambrose attempted to run, picking up his last book from the library on the way, but by then the gangster had caught him, demanding to know where the 'evidence' was stashed. Ambrose fought back surprisingly hard; he was not about to lose his chance to escape all of this. During the fight the attacker reached for the nearest weapon, the bronze bookend and knocked Ambrose out cold....or so he thought, until he checked and found that Ambrose wasn't breathing.

Deciding it was time to get out, and fast, the killer looked up at the door to see Jimmy staring in at the scene in the hall. Jimmy fled, in terror, racing back to get the chest and try to getaway alone but the gangster caught him. There could be no witnesses. The bookend was in the gangster's pocket; he had intended to dispose of it but poor Jimmy met the same fate as Ambrose.

Fearing he was about to caught, the gangster scarpered, throwing the weapon in to the undergrowth. He would have kicked himself if he knew that he had missed a little treasure trove there in the wood.

Jimmy wasn't the only witness to Ambrose's death. Geraldine had watched it all in horror although she didn't know then that Jimmy was also involved. She sat up for the next few hours, trying to come to terms with what she had set in motion, and waited for the discovery of Ambrose's body and the ensuing drama. She eventually saw poor Bunty arrive to work and make the grim discovery. There was nothing for it now but Plan B. Her reduced assets were going to have to do. She had started some weeks ago, with Sean's help, to put her remaining money beyond the reach of the Irish justice system, just in case, and had to hope it would be enough. He knew the ropes; he was in the same process, in fact, and hinted to her that he had always enjoyed his trips to Dubai where he had a couple of friends in the same 'game' as himself. One must have a Plan B!

***

As Geraldine was planning her hasty departure, others were also making plans. Some hours after she had discovered Ambrose in the library, Bunty dashed up to Rory in his care home. She was familiar to the staff as a frequent visitor to poor Mr. Carthusian. Such a loyal employee. She often took him for little walks in the grounds and occasionally even took him for a drive to break the monotony. Rory and Barbara, now Bunty, had a long professional history dealing in the world of rare books and each had skills that complemented those of the other.

Rory had connections all over the world in the legitimate and less than legitimate world of trade in valuable artefacts. He knew the brokers and the buyers who were prepared to turn a blind eye to provenance

For the thrill of possessing the rarest of artefacts, mostly books in Rory's case. Rare masterpieces were often used in the criminal underworld as collateral and could also be ransomed

to insurers for massive sums.

Rory's contacts and Barbara's skill in creative accounting and the dark arts of hiding money had made them the perfect team. Of course, there were great risks attached to this trade, as each of them had come to realise. In Rory's case he had run foul of the Dublin gangs and Barbara had had to make a dash from Saudi when her substitution of the Rothchild Prayer book looked like being uncovered. She did not yet know if that had happened because the then owner wouldn't have been in a position to report such a crime in case it lifted the lid on his own murky dealings.

When Barbara came back from Saudi, she had set about constructing a life that looked nothing like her previous one. She was sure that sooner or later, her deception would catch up with her and she could be found. Her new identity needed to be radically different, at least until the time came when she felt could make another move and liquidate her precious asset. Moving in with Benny had certainly achieved that!

When she had sorted that out, she got in touch with Rory. She knew he could find a buyer for the Prayerbook. It could fetch several million dollars. She was so surprised and upset to discover that Rory had been diagnosed with dementia and was now living in the care home, even if it was more like a luxurious hotel.

It took a little while for her to cotton on to the truth; when he decided he would trust her, she found that he was as sharp as ever, though paranoid about being found out. He felt that he was relatively safe in the home and it was luxurious, but really, the pretense was becoming too much. He would end up really demented if he didn't get out.

Rory was very concerned too about what was going on in Beacon Court. Angela and Mitzi wouldn't listen to him. They knew that he didn't have dementia, but they were taking advantage of his situation to do as they thought fit. They had him over a barrel. He had no control anymore as they had secured enduring power of attorney due to his diagnosis!

He did manage to persuade them to give poor Bunty McGilligan a job as cleaner; the poor woman had worked in his office at one time and had fallen on hard times. She was a great worker, he said, and he could vouch for her total discretion. Bunty, alias Barbara, was his only source of information now in Beacon Court and he had been increasingly disturbed by what he was hearing. It sounded chaotic with all sorts of sinister visitors causing the other residents to feel frightened, complaining to the Guards and drawing attention to the place.

Well, now his worst fears had been realized. The twins and their boorish boyfriends had made a total mess of everything. It couldn't have gone more horribly wrong. He and Barbara needed to have a long and careful conversation in private. She dropped into the Residence Manager to say that she was just taking Mr. Carthusian out for some fresh air.

***

What a stroke of luck for D.I O'Donnell and D.S. King! The wooden chest and its contents had surfaced just in time. O'Donnell and King were coming under unrelenting pressure from the Super and his bosses. The Super seemed almost unhinged these days whatever had gotten into him! The interviews with the residents of Beacon Court were yielding very little, if any, useful information. As with Bunty, Ellen and Carrie were sure that most of them were hiding something but they couldn't quite find their way into the real story. The contents of the chest,

The Secrets of Beacon Court particularly the USB stick would hopefully crack the case open. Of course, the files on the stick were password protected but it would only be a matter of time before the Garda Technical Bureau found their way in. Meanwhile, forensics would carry on in Beacon Court, looking for evidence of the murderer and for a match for the fingerprints on the murder weapon.

Angela and Mitzi were not in any state yet to be re-interviewed. They seemed to be falling apart as the reality set in. They were also dealing with the boys' families and friends, waiting for postmortems to be done before they could arrange for funerals. Sean would not divulge anything without legal protection. He was spending long hours in his office in town and hadn't been seen around the place for a while

Most of the other residents appeared frightened, with Effie and Kitty reluctant to leave their apartments until the murders were solved. Geraldine had taken it badly and would not even answer the door.

Peter Portius was the only one coming and going, unfazed by what had happened and taking a keen interest in what the forensic team were up to.

***

Dublin Airport Terminal Two was so much nicer than Terminal One, Geraldine thought to herself. She was through security and waiting for her flight to London where she would make her connection to Male in the Maldives.

Her head was spinning with the events of the last few days, indeed weeks, but she would have plenty of time to sort it all out later. For now, she needed to get a drink, relax a bit, and stay focused on the journey ahead.

It was hard to believe that this day had finally come but there was no turning back.

As she sipped her Scotch on ice, she began to unwind but then sat bolt upright, wondering if she was seeing things. Was that Bunty McGilligan the cleaner from Beacon Court? She looked very different if so, quite sophisticated, with flawless makeup and a very expensive looking coat.

Maybe it wasn't her but looking closer it actually was Bunty. And who was that stylish, distinguished looking man she was with? Geraldine had heard that Bunty lived a miserable life with a hopeless, drunken partner. What was going on? Where were they going?

The London flight was called; it was ready to board. She had to go. The following day, after a long, intense and complex session with the Garda technical bureau and serious crime experts, O'Donnell and King were left utterly astounded. The data on the stick was almost too extraordinary to take in. Angela, Mitzi, Ambrose, Jimmy, Sean....money laundering for drugs gangs, forgery of rare books, fraudulent trading on the stock market! This was so much bigger than anything Oldchurch Gardai would normally handle. Several divisions of the Gardai were now on the case. The urgent local tasks now were to secure search warrants for the apartments and court orders to freeze bank accounts. O'Donnell and King were to head to Beacon Court with uniformed Garda backup to bring the suspects, so far, Angela, Mitzi and Salinger into the station.

They would then go looking for Bunty.

When they got to Beacon Court in the early evening, it was getting dark and the place looked deserted. Angela and Mitzi were out, Effie and Kitty were in Effie's sitting room still soothing their nerves with the aid of more than a couple of little brandies.

They had no knowledge of anyone else's whereabouts. Geraldine wasn't answering the door, they said. Sean seemed to be working round the clock in town, and Angela and Mitzi had presumably gone down the country, maybe to be with the

Ambrose and Jimmy's families? Effie and Kitty had looked for them this morning to see why Bunty, the cleaner had not shown up. With all the traffic through the place in the last few days, it was filthy!

Bloody hell! What was going on here? O'Donnell and King were unnerved; they each had a very bad feeling about this. It looked as though they were going to come away empty handed. As they pondered their next move, Peter Portius arrived, rushing through the hall, accompanied by the postman! What on earth was going on now?

Grim-faced, Portius came straight over to O'Donnell; 'We have to talk, it's urgent!'

The Secrets of Beacon Court

Lotta Vokes

The Secrets of Beacon Court

So there we are … the book is done,
with the chosen denouement chapter
written by
Edel O'Kennedy
having been added.

But that is not all; the denouement
chapters submitted by other authors now
follow
Maybe you would have chosen one of
them.
It's 'chacun a son gout' time, so read on
for your continuing entertainment.

Lotta Vokes

CHAPTER TWELVE

Natalie Cox

Bunty watched through the window of Geraldine Haven's apartment as she saw the forensics team swarm the undergrowth at the back of Beacon Court.

She felt a small shudder of fear, an emotion not familiar to her. And she remembered once, while reading a book by Patricia Highsmith called 'Ripley Under Water', about a sociopath, who had questioned her own personality.

But Bunty, never one to linger, had passed her fear off as her parents' fault.

She passed off a lot of her culpabilities and shortcomings as her parents' responsibility. Why would she not,

143

she thought? She'd been given to her grandmother as a six-week-old as a payment for inheritance. Well, that's how Bunty saw it. Her grandmother wanted a girl and she got one, Elisabeth Carthusian. Her grandparents changed her name from Elizabeth to Penelope, shortened it to 'Bunty', and then pretended she was adopted, a belief she herself held until she was sixteen. But she was really a Carthusian in every fiber of her being and what was rightfully hers, she would have. A secret she may be, but invisible she is not!

Wasn't it sad that Jimmy was dead, Bunty caustically thought to herself, while remembering him as a useless crook? The crook part did not bother her, but his incompetence did.

Geraldine Haven entered the room interrupting Bunty's thoughts. "What is going on out there?" Geraldine quipped. "Not sure Ms. Haven," Bunty replied, as she continued dusting the old Edwardian oak roll top desk.

Geraldine watched out the window for a few moments before a knock came to the door.

Bunty listened intensely as she recognized the voice of Detective Sergeant Carrie King. She heard her say that Mr. Jimmy Hennessy had been found dead under suspicious circumstances. "Oh Lord" she heard Geraldine Haven say while inviting the detective in.

King stepped in and, on seeing Bunty, remarked "oh nice to see you again Mrs. McGilligan".

"You too, dear" replied Bunty, while attempting to exit the room.

"Just a minute Mrs. McGilligan" snapped King. "There is a second dead man in the grounds of this building within a matter of two days and I need a statement from all of you".

Geraldine sighed heavily, appearing utterly tired and exasperated with the whole situation. "Shall I make some coffee?" she asked.

King willingly agreed, much to Bunty's contempt, knowing they would now be alone for the twenty minutes it would take Geraldine to swallow two Xanax tablets and manage her coffee machine that looked like something from the starship enterprise.

"Did you know Jimmy Hennessy, or see him often? King asked.

"No" Bunty responded. "I have met him of course, nice fella, always said

'Hello'. Gave me a nice bottle of red wine last Christmas. Mitzi will be devastated. What a disaster, and a coincidence too.".

"Yes" King said, looking around the room. 'Bunty', she said, with a lengthy emphasis on both name and eye contact. We will need you to come to the station tomorrow for a formal statement.

"Me" Bunty retorted, "why"?

"Not just you, Bunty, but we have some questions that have arisen from an important piece of intelligence, and we need to speak to you in more detail to clarify some minor details".

"Oh", I see "well I have to work. What time?"

"8 a.m. in Oldchurch Gardai station".

Bunty knew by King's tone that she was not being flippant, and willingly agreed, with her usual gullible manner. She noted she was no longer being called "Mrs. McGilligan", but "Bunty".

When Geraldine arrived back at the room, Bunty made her excuses and left.

Now fear had shrouded her, and she was in fight or flight mode. What to do? What did they know? King knows something and Bunty knew it. She hopped in her car, wondering whether to pack a bag and run. Where, where could she go? maybe grab her Bible and disappear, but Bunty had no passport or money.

Her money was a book, a book worth millions, on the verge of being sold by two stupid fools whom she'd trusted to know the right people. Six million due into her bank account. Now two dead ducks. 'Jesus Christ!, she thought, what a mess! No, she would have to stay and come up with a strategy. "Damn those two morons Finnegan and Hennessy!" she thought. "Pathetic, bloody useless!"

Bunty arrived home, petted her dog, scowled at the drunken, sleeping Benny. She went upstairs, got her bible, and wrapped it in velvet fabric, covered it in tinfoil and black bags, then sealed it with tape. Bunty then got back into the car and drove to Devil's Glen woods.

It was dark and cold, and she was shaking with fear, not from the dark though! It was from her earlier brief discussion with King. Bunty walked to a tree where she often sat, buried the book and quickly drove home.

I need to sell this book, she was thinking, right away! But how?

Her only hopes of doing so were dead! ……Bunty knew she had a problem!

King spoke with Geraldine for some time about the goings on in Beacon Court and about the people who frequented it. King was not sure if Geraldine was very tired or had been drinking but thought it better to take a formal statement in the coming days.

Before leaving, King asked Geraldine about Bunty. "How long has Bunty McGilligan worked here?"

Geraldine said "Years, but I'm not sure how many".

King asked how well she knew Bunty and Geraldine said, "very well, she is a lovely lady, a real salt of the earth type".

King mumbled something vague to Geraldine and left.

Geraldine thought 'what a strange question' but decided not to ponder it. The only thing she wanted to ponder was estate agents and her bed. "What a strange place, full of strange people", she thought, as she checked every lock and window. God knows what will happen tomorrow, she mused, as she got into bed and turned off the lights.

Back in Oldchurch Garda station the wooden chest was in Kings office with three gardai standing around it. They were waiting for permission to bag the contents for forensics, secretly all a little fearful of opening it. King was tired, but her conversation with Downes earlier had irked her. The information from Peter Portius, although not evidenced, could be the crux of this mess. Who would have thought that two ordinary or semi-ordinary men were involved with the importation and/or aiding and abetting of a criminal gang? One of the most prominent families this side of the city and this was what they were involved with. Who knew what? That, was the problem! and who was the ringleader? Who the hell had murdered those two fools? "God forgive me" she thought to herself, "they are somebodies' sons!"

Bunty though! This was disconcerting, Portius had uncovered that Bunty had lived in Saudi and was not a cleaner, or anything close.

He had also revealed that dear little Bunty had left Saudi with some immensely powerful people looking for her and specifically, her luggage and what it contained. Could it be connected to this? King had a strong gut feeling and she did not like it.

The Secrets of Beacon Court

"Ok lads" she said "let us get this open. Glove up, it is going to be a long night" she said.

Bunty tossed and turned, surveying every aspect of where it had all gone wrong. What loomed ahead for her in Oldchurch Garda station tomorrow morning. She feared for her future. Bunty always had a scheme, but this time was different, her opportunities were constrained.

King yanked open the chest with a distinct feeling of dread in her stomach. To her wonder it contained a lot of paperwork, neatly filed in chronological order. What were they? She thought. Some appeared in foreign languages, Arabic, Chinese Japanese, which, she was not sure! The Gardai started to bag them for forensics. John Mc Govern, a local Community Garda, noticed they were stamped, denoting that they were appraisals for books.

"Wow!" he exclaimed, "expensive ones too." King told him to "get on with it, this is evidence." She noticed a brown envelope, carefully opening it.

It was a birth certificate for an Elizabeth Carthusian. Mm, she thought ...., maybe this is finally the evidence we need.

Could Portius have been correct? Was there another Carthusian seeking revenge? Damn it, King thought, it's Bunty 'Bloody' McGilligan.

King left the room and phoned Superintendent Downes. Awakening Downes from his slumber was never a pleasurable experience. "What?" He responded.

"Sorry Skipper" King countered, "Peter Portis was right, there is another Carthusian and I'm almost certain it's Bunty McGilligan".

"Really?" Downes said, "ok let us put what we have to her in the morning. Go home King" he said, "it has been a long day."

'For some of us,' King thought.

Bunty arose from a sleepless night. It was 6.30 a.m. as she went downstairs and put her beloved dog outside before feeding him. She made herself a coffee and lit her first cigarette of the day. She looked at the kitchen counter covered in used dishes and empty bottles of gin. Going upstairs, she picked out her best 'Bunty the Cleaner' outfit, an ill-fitting navy-blue dress and black, flat, lace up shoes. No makeup, I need to look as vulnerable as possible, she thought.

Bunty looked in the mirror and patted her hair flat, when suddenly, she started to cry, not small tears or tears of self-pity but tears that came from a place she had never known existed, from the depths of her soul. Her body was screaming, filled with poignant, emotional distress. It felt somewhat from a torture chamber.

Bunty could not move; she was frozen in disbelief and shock. In all her fifty-three years, she could not remember a tear leaving her eye. She fell on her bed curled up in the fetal position, as every memory of her parents' rejection hit her. Sadness seeped from her body, her mind, her heart, her soul and it frightened her, but in a bizarre way she could not fight it, she could not even challenge it. Bunty had to finally succumb. She lay there feeling something she had never experienced before in her life, a lightness. She could not understand it but knew she had not time to either analyze or consider it.

Bunty grabbed her handbag went downstairs, stood looking at Benny for a minute, then she woke him up from his sleep, as usual, on the chair. He looked at her in surprise,

"Benny" Bunty said, "You are a good man and I'm sorry." Benny looked surprised, but with that, Bunty had walked out the door. It was 7.30 and Bunty was heading to Oldchurch but opted to detour. There was one last person she wanted to see before she met King.

Bunty pulled into Rosemount Nursing home at 7:45 and asked to see

Rory Carthusian. The lady on duty appeared to take pity on Bunty, a probable combination of her red eyes and exhausted appearance.

She walked into Rory Carthusian's room, knowing he had dementia. Regardless, there were conversations that had never happened and never would, but Bunty wanted to see him. He was thin and frail and quiet, lying there staring at nothing. Bunty expected to feel resentment and fury, but she felt nothing but understanding. "Rory," she said.

He looked at her, seemingly confused.

"I am Elizabeth your daughter." Rory looked more intently at her. Bunty had to hold back tears for the second time in one morning. "Elizabeth" he said, "Oh Elizabeth, I think of you every day."

Bunty knew there was no point in asking the whys? She gently kissed his forehead and rubbed his hand. "I missed my dad," she whispered, noticing tears in his eyes. With that Bunty turned and left, knowing she would never lay eyes on her father again. As Bunty went to leave, she observed the deserted medicine trolley. Like a professional she took four boxes of Codamol and popped them in her handbag.

King and Downes sat in the station with Peter Portius and a shiny copy of Elizabeth Carthusian's birth certificate. All watching the clock; 8.45 a.m. and no Bunty! King was worried, maybe she should have arrested her last night.

Bunty left Rosemount Nursing home, and headed to her favorite tree in Devil's Glen woods, where she dug up her

159

precious fortune, put it into an envelope addressed to Ahmad Khan, Al Muhammadiyah, Riyadh, Saudi Arabia. He was getting it back. She left the post office with an uncommon feeling of calm, got into her little Yaris, lit a cigarette, checked her handbag to ensure everything was in order and took off not quite sure where to go somewhere West perhaps. Or at the very least somewhere quiet and peaceful. She really wasn't sure, but it would not be Oldchurch Garda station, of that she was certain.

CHAPTER TWELVE

by Annie Devine

So, Ambrose was going to turn on the girls. I was keeping a close eye on him. When I confronted him that morning, he was incoherent, I told him how pathetic he was and how he wasn't good enough for My Girls.

But how did he get his hands on the chest? The damned chest: Rory and I should have buried it years ago …. But then again… Why??? I want them to know my Family Secrets. I want them to appreciate all that I have done for them. Scrubbing toilets, polishing brass, dusting floors always in the shadow. And for what? Because they are My children…

Lotta Vokes

Those two babies were mine... I remember when they were born, Kate just whisked them out of the hospital.

I swore to Rory how I would be there for those twins forever and I would remain silent, how I would protect our legacy. We always knew Kate would marry Rory; she was 12 years older than me. My parents were pathetically groveling towards Rory and his parents, but it was I who knew the real Rory.

I was sent away to have the twins and Kate made Rory swear I would be no part of hers or the twins' life ever again... But Rory and I were in love, stayed in love despite the fact I remained in the midlands laundry for four years after the births of Angela, and Mitzi .

Rory arranged for me to move to the Middle East, where I was groomed and

The Secrets of Beacon Court

gradually learned what it is to be a member of an international Drug Cartel. Saudi was a learning curve, I'll admit that. Rory was well respected there because it was known he was from one of the most powerful conglomerates in the entire world. It was when the Sheik made an unwelcome remark towards me, that it was 'Good-bye Saudi' and back to Ireland as his lover. And then Rory, you opted out. The only thing I ever agreed on with the Cartel was getting rid of Kate – she needed to die.

You took your retirement; you acted crazy and eased yourself out while you lured me in. Second in command you said, watch the twins you said, and oh yes, indeed I did.

Ambrose was a fool. He thought that he could conspire against my family and WIN! So, I stopped him. I met him in the hall. He was drunk. I was waiting. I told him that I knew what he was trying to do. To steal the business that my family had built. To take what was ours …. He told me to get out. He offered to give me a priceless book. He begged me to take it and go away. I took the book naturally; it was only worth a few million, nice hard binding though.

He thought that I would go away if he gave me a book worth a few million Euro! One book through the base of the skull later, Ambrose was no longer a fool. In fact, Ambrose was no longer alive.

I left his body lying face down. When I slipped out the door, I didn't expect to meet Jimmy. I thought he was so predictable, but that morning he arrived at 5.30, stumbling up the avenue singing New York, New York. I knew he saw me.

Although it was dark, I set off the sensor light, so I spoke to him and asked if he would help me pick fresh daffodils for the entrance hall. He obliged.

I held the book firmly in my hand as I lead the way to the garden, he wasn't coherent enough to realize we were going in the wrong direction… I knew what I was about to do. So, I confronted him and told him I knew about his underhanded plan with Ambrose. His demeanor changed immediately. It didn't take long for his festering domineering personality to appear. He challenged me; his condescending tone was barely audible. I was intolerant listening to his drivel, so I wedged that book into his skull. Gratifying. By the way, I don't mind murder. I find it invigorating.

***

Lotta Vokes

Oldchurch Station was never busier when I was interviewed. I knew the detectives were pretty incompetent but was relieved when six days after the finding of Jimmy, Sean Salinger was arrested and charged with double murder.

As for me ... I'm just disembarking. Oh, the balmy air. The heat. Buenos Aires. Anything can happen in this heat with a few billion in the bank. Anything. My work is finally done and my life has begun. I assume Benny will wonder where I went but I suspect he will miss the dog more than me.

I choose not to look back, but into the future instead, yet I wonder how safe Rory and I are here ....

CHAPTER TWELVE

By Alan Grainger

As Carrie and Ellen raced down to the wooded area where the body had been found, hoping to get there before the box was opened, a huge black Lexus came through the gate and drove up to the front door of the house.

As it went by, they could see the driver was a big man with silvery grey hair. He didn't look particularly familiar, so they stood aside and simply nodded a greeting as he passed. When he climbed out of the car at the front door steps, and strode round to the house's impressive entrance though, they got a better look at him ... but he still didn't seem familiar so, when he reached for the big brass door knocker, they continued on their way down to the crowd of people they'd seen in the trees, down by the gate, and looking at something lying on the ground.

***

Bunty McGlligan opened the door in response to the man's knock. And she nearly dropped when she saw who had summoned her. He never said a word; he simply pushed past her and barged into the building.

She made no attempt to stop him; just stood back, open mouthed, and let him pass. 'Jesus,' she said as he did so, 'you're the last person I expected to see when I opened the door … how are you Mr Carthusian?'

'How are you Mr Carthusian?' he mimicked. 'Don't think you can butter me up with pathetic expressions of sympathy. Pack up your stuff and get out of my sight you … you old bag … and don't come back here again if you value your life. I know what you've been up to, always did, but when I worked out you were only messing with small stuff and keeping clear of my contacts … I left you alone. If you'd been satisfied with what you were pulling in when I went into the care home, and stuck with that instead of trying to muscle in on my network, you'd have been alright.'

'But … '

'But me no 'Buts' Bunty McGlligan. Did you not hear me, y'ould bitch? You're finished here, no more using the pretext of being our cleaner so you could see what we we're up to … you're done … now get out of my sight and don't come back … I've few more scores to settle this morning and I want you out of my life first.'

The expression on Bunty's face hardened. 'You don't know what's happened do you, you daft old so and so. There's been a murder here … no … two murders. Did you not see the Garda car? They're crawlin' all over the place looking for clues … your daughters' fancy men have 'kicked the bucket'. And good riddance; they were goin' through your money like a hot knife through butter and the girls couldn't stop 'em. Wasters, both of them, those two young men … eighteen carat wasters. They were getting away with murder, so they were; Ambrose and Jimmy. But not now … oh no - now it's the other way round.'

'Bunty, if you don't stop waffling and get out of my sight, I'll not be responsible for what happens to you. Now clear off and don't come back … ever!'

'Oh … don't worry … I'm not staying … I wouldn't be caught dead here.'

'You will if you are not gone in the next half hour.' Carthusian barked. 'Now get out of my way.'

As Mrs McGlligan disappeared into the back lobby, Carthusian swung round to shut the door but, when he went to reach for it, he saw that a woman was mounting the steps. It was Detective Inspector Ellen O'Donnell.

'Sorry Sir,' she said. 'You shouldn't be in here … this a crime scene; we're investigating an incident that took place here yesterday. What's the nature of your business?'

'The nature of my business Miss 'er Miss ...'

'Detective Inspector.' O'Donnell answered bluntly, taking out her warrant card and showing it to him.

'A female detective eh? That's surely a first ... you look too young to be a sleuth ... you look more like a ...'

'What is your business here, Sir?' O'Donnell repeated.

Carthusian smiled. 'You don't know who I am do you? I'm Rory Carthusian, I own this damned house.'

'Oh ... 'er ... sorry, Sir ... we were told the owner lived in a nursing home and that he was suffering from dementia.'

'Which is correct; I *did* suffer as you say ... and I *have* been living in a sheltered housing complex in Dundrum. But then my daughters heard of this new treatment in America, and they managed to get hold of some the magic drug they were told would cure it by using an old contact of mine in the New York.

I'd only been on it for two days when the improvements started to come through. Now, just a fortnight later, I'm free of my problem completely; cured and ready to rock and roll.

So can I carry on upstairs? I want to see my daughters; I understand they've both been bereaved.'

'It's an odd way of putting it but, yes, I suppose you could call it that.' said O'Donnell, 'I think it'd be better if I brought you round to the back door though; the forensic team are still not finished down here'

'Ah,' said Carthusian, his eyes darting round the room. 'so is this where the ... 'er ... the 'er ... the incident I heard about took place?

'It is, yes ... just there.' O'Donnell replied, pointing to the blood stain on the floor where Ambrose had been found. 'That's where your daughter's friend was lying. He'd been hit on the head with something heavy, an ornamental bronze bookend we think. It must have killed him almost instantly.'

As they spoke, they slowly walked out through the front door and round to the rear of the house; entering it by the conservatory that sheltered the back door. Carthusian shoved O'Donnell to one side when they were inside, and pushed forward to embrace Angela, who'd turned when she'd heard her father's voice.

'Oh Dad,' she whispered, just loud enough for the policewomen to hear,

174

'you'll never guess what happened here yesterday.'

O'Donnell, pretending she wasn't listening, thought that odd. Why had Angela expressed no surprise at finding her father in Beacon Court instead of his home in Dundrum, the place he'd been living in for the previous four years. She said nothing though.

'Mitzi's upstairs,' said Angela. 'I'll give her a buzz and ask her to join us in my apartment.'

Carthusian nodded. 'Thank you, Inspector.' He said, as he turned back to face the two uniformed guards who'd been talking to Angela when he arrived.

'No problem,' O'Donnell replied. 'I'll tell the Super you're here; he'll want a word with you.'

'Yeah, yeah … that's OK; I'll be up in … 'er … where'll we go Angela?' 'We'll be in my place, which is just off the hall, Inspector;' she answered, 'I'll take Dad through now and we can collect Mitzi on the way.'

O'Donnell glanced at her watch. 'Fair enough,' she said. She'd been half expecting the Superintendent to come looking for her, but one of the other Guards had told her, a few minutes earlier, that he'd gone back to the barracks. So, while Rory Carthusian was talking with his daughters and suggesting a plan to get their empire back on its tracks, O'Donnell walked down to the trees by the gate to see what was happening.

***

'What d'you think's in it.' D.S. King asked, struggling to pass the heavy box to O'Donnell, who tried to guess-weigh it.

'Not a clue … I see you've forced it … was there no key?'

'No.' We waited for you and, when we saw you walking down the drive, we pried open the lock … but we didn't look inside much … we just riffled through the papers on the top, shall I look deeper?'

'Yes, go on,' said, O'Donnell, 'but be careful. Under those papers there could be a money hoard or a load of drugs, and we don't want to destroy, damage or lose anything.'

They all crowded round to see what was in the box but, deep as they dug into it, it only contained the pieces of paper; certificates of some sort and, for most of those watching with great anticipation, their faces fell.

Not O'Donnell's though … she knew what those bits of paper were in an instant … they were Bearer Bonds, thousands and thousands of dollars' worth of bearer bonds, exchangeable at any bank once identification had been established - a fortune in a box.

But whose bonds were they? And what was Angela's man, Jimmy, doing with them down in the woods? Was he intending to hide them by burying them for someone else to collect? Or was he squirreling them away to be redeemed later by himself?

Most important of all, though, were the bonds his?'

King didn't have to think twice; she guessed straight off. 'Drugs! I'll bet it's drugs money he had to get out of sight knowing that, as a result of Ambrose's death, we'll be into every nook and cranny looking for anything that might explain it. He wanted this stuff completely out of our sight … and what better way to do that than bury it? Look, it's obvious, this death, and that of Ambrose, who took the hit some time yesterday, are about drugs, money, and jealousy.

I'll bet we find one or two of the others living in this house are, in one way or another, also involved in crookery of some sort which, bearing in mind the book we found beside Ambrose's body, might include forgery of old books and manuscripts. This lot may not have been on *our* horizon but then … well you know how it is as far as the drug squad are concerned; they tell us nothing, they think we're all plods.' There was head shaking all round as she spoke; each of the guards there had been shoved to one side by the Drug Squad at one time or another … and they resented it.

'What about the weapon you said you'd found?' asked O'Donnell.

'You mean this?' asked a guard, who was holding a transparent bag with what looked like a bronze bookend inside it. 'I think there's some dried blood on it.' he added, 'as well as what looks like head hairs. It's a fearsome weapon … feel the weight of it.'

As they were speaking it started to rain, and there was a rush by everyone to get back the house; everyone except the two Guards who were left to get soaked as they flung a waterproof sheet over the area where the box had been found.

The Secrets of Beacon Court

When they got back to the house, O'Donnell asked Angela if she'd move in with Mitzi for a day or two so they could use her room for interviewing. Angela said she would, and soon it was fixed with King, at O'Donnell's behest, lining up the residents, the cleaner and the postman, and all to be spoken to.

Hardly had they started than O'Donnell whispered; 'Watch out 'Up and Downes' is on his way. I just saw him drawing up at the steps.

King smiled. 'The Super? … Good … I need to ask him a few questions he won't be expecting; I want to see him squirm the way he's had me squirming before now.'

As soon as he entered the room, Downes was roaring. 'What the hell have you been doing all morning. The fecking' perpetrators of these crimes'll be miles away by now ... miles away; there's no chance we'll get 'em.'

O'Donnell, furious at the accusation, smiled. 'We have the weapon, and we've found a large sum of money. *I reckon* we we've been progressing quite nicely. Look Sir ... I'm about to start on second interviews with the sisters and the other residents, d'you want to join in?

'Join in? What sort of question is that? It's about time you and I had a little chat. And you Inspector,' he said, turning to King, 'go and find us a cup of tea while I try to coax an update, however far-fetched, from D.I. O'Donnell.'

King was seething, but she knew protesting about the Super's bullying tactics would get them nowhere, so she gritted her teeth and did what he asked.

182

O'Donnell, equally infuriated, launched into a brief resume of horrific events of the previous night and then began to detail her response to it. 'I've conducted preliminary interviews with most of the residents of the house, and this is what I've found out. The building has seven flats in it, of which two belong to the owner's daughters - Angela and Mitzi Carthusian. Each has, 'er …. no … *had*, a man living with her, and it's these two men who have been murdered. Both women have been high flyers in the past but, I gather, they're not as well off as they used to be, and they've been blaming the two men for it. The family have been 'big in hardwood timber' for generations. Mostly it is mahogany, which they import from the West Indies; and the trade was worth millions until recently. At their peak, five years ago, Mrs Carthusian, the twins' mother, was killed in a car accident in Bray … and it was as though their tap had been turned off. Rory, the head of the family, a man who was as strong as an ox physically, went downhill mentally and, within a year, he was in a nursing home suffering from dementia.

The girls tried to carry on the business but the company, Tropical Hardwoods, was the sort of enterprise that needs a strong policy maker to lead it. Rory Carthusian was such a person but, unable to bear the grief of losing his wife, he deteriorated very rapidly.

Before a year was out, he'd 'given up' and appeared to make no effort to resist the onslaught of dementia. For several years now, he's been living in sheltered accommodation in Dundrum, leaving his daughters to run the business which he had cleverly broadened out into some very fishy channels - drugs, money laundering, fake art work, and so on. And that's what they've been doing … running it and ruining it at the same time.

With nobody to control them, the girls went wild; spending money on ventures and adventures as though they'd never have another opportunity to do so. When they brought the two men, Ambrose and Jimmy, into their lives, the company's slide downhill accelerated. Now, I believe, the legal elements of it are heading for liquidation.

During this period, Ambrose and Jimmy tried every trick in the book to prize the business from the girls. Not only did they rob them they …'

Downes held up his hand as though he was controlling traffic. 'Wait a minute, wait a minute.' He said, 'How do you know all this?'

'Mrs McGlligan, the cleaner; she told me. It's astonishing what she knows.'

'The cleaner? So much for loyalty … that woman's been here for yonks. I've often …'

'What … seen her? So, you know the family do you Sir; I hadn't realised.'

'No,' Downes said, hesitatingly, 'It's just that …'

O'Donnell smiled. 'Yes … I can see things falling into place now. I'd never have guessed you had any sort of connection with the weird lot of people living here, but now I reckon it explains some of the wilder accusations that came out during the preliminary interviews.'

The superintendent laughed, 'Like what?'

'Like … Sorry Sir, this sounds stupid I know but 'erm … like you were involved in some crooked business with the Carthusians.'

'Me with them, oh for Goodness's sake.'

'And others.'

'Others? Doing what?'

'Importing, cutting and selling narcotics, faking artwork and stealing it.

"Has Walt Disney got something to do with this?'

"Huh. Sounds like it; I said it was stupid.'

'Me messing with drugs and stolen artwork? You're off your head.'

'And, I heard there are a number of international enforcement agencies after you. In fact, I understand they're here already.'

'Rubbish ... like which ones?'

'Like the one Mr Salinger works for - Europol.'

'Salinger? Don't make me laugh; he's just a bloody crook. He tried to get me involved a financial racket he was in, but I gave him short shrift.'

'And did you do the same to Peter Portius ... ignore him? He told me he's here on behalf of another hush hush outfit; not that I believed him.'

'Hush hush ... There you go again ... what are you talking about?'

'Interpol I think, or was it Mossad?'

'Good God ... Europol ... Interpol ... Mossad ... what next? Why not the KGB and the CIA? Look, Inspector, 'I've had enough of this. You can peddle your silly stories wherever you like; you'll find nothing to connect me to any of them.'

'As you wish, Sir,' O'Donnell replied, trying not to grin. 'I'll be putting my report in tomorrow anyway but, in view of what I've been told regarding your connection with the Carthusians, I'm going to have to send it to the Deputy Commissioner direct, you know the drill. I can't get over how lucky it was that the first person I spoke to was Mrs McGlligan. Now, if I can find a match for the fingerprints discovered on the weapon, the heavy bronze book end we've now got, I reckon I'll have the killer of both men.'

'Well, you won't find my fingerprints on your damned bookend.' Said Downes, rising to leave. 'It'll be *you* for the high jump if you send that report in; I'm calling the Assistant Commissioner myself the minute I get back, so you'd better check your facts.'

As soon as the Superintendent had gone, King came back in. 'The tea's cold, shall I make another?'

'Yeah. Why not?'

'Hey, that was some session you had with 'his nibs' from what I could hear through the wall.'

O'Donnell grinned. 'It's just the start. Listen to this; I got a preliminary report from forensic just before the Super arrived. I now know who did it … the only recent prints on the bronze bookend belong to that French guy, Mr 'Allo 'Allo.'

'Really? He hinted he was with one of the 'pols' when we were talking earlier, what a liar.'

'Oh he's that alright. And there's more … he was seen slipping out the back gate of Beacon House an hour ago and he had a very suspicious load of …'

"Back gate? I never noticed one."

"Well there actually is, and it leads onto Puck's Castle lane. Anyway, he had this rucksack of old books on his back … very old books; valuable ones by the look of 'em, I'm told.'

'So where is he now?' King asked.

'Locked up in a holding cell in Bray. They'll hang onto him until the morning, despite his protests.'

'So what d'you think he actually is, if he was bluffing about being employed by the spooks, and what sort of a sentence will he get if we can prove him guilty?'

O'Donnell shook her head. 'I've no idea whether his connection to the secret service outfits mentioned is real, but for a double murder …. twenty years.'

"For each killing?"

"He could get more but a good chunk of it would probably be remitted. I can't see the logic in that."

'Forty years! Phew! That's some sentence. Even allowing for remission he's going to be in jail for the rest of his life.'

O'Donnell could stop a grin forming. 'And all that time on meat and two veg; he won't like that.'

King began to splutter ... 'On no ... of course he won't. It'll be worse than the guillotine for him, what with him being a Frenchman and used to all manner of fancy foods. No, he won't care much for the Haute Cuisine stodge they serve up in Arbour Hill Prison, will he?'

'And d'you know what?' O'Donnell answered, as tears of laughter

192

The Secrets of Beacon Court

began trickling down her cheeks. 'The only frog's legs he's going to see while he's in there will be his own!'

'You've got a point there.' Said King. 'Anyway … Vive La France.'

'How about Vive le Gin and Tonic' O'Donnell answered, 'Come on, I've had enough for today; the Frenchman's going nowhere so let's relax for a while. My place is just down the road, and my neighbours will be assembling on the terrace with their bottles and glasses. Let's join them.

'Yeees.' Said King … Why not?'

CHAPTER TWELVE

Mary Cait Hermon

The two detectives made their way to the lab to see what the techs had discovered, Ellen refusing to fill Carrie in until she had seen for herself. Donovan's team, alongside an expert in the field, was gathered around the chest which had been discovered in the woods.

They stood back when Ellen and Carrie entered the lab, creating space for them both at the table on which the chest stood.

"Is it true?" asked Ellen. "Are you one hundred percent certain?"

Donovan's expert nodded, a big grin on his face.

194

"What? Certain of what?" asked Carrie, looking between the two, and then down at the contents of the chest. It looked like a pile of old books to her, what was unbelievable about that?

"Carrie, do you know what this is?" asked Ellen, pointing to a red leather book decorated with gold. Carrie shook her head. "The Rothschild Prayerbook, the *actual* prayerbook. It's one of the most important manuscripts of the Flemish Renaissance. It's worth millions!" Ellen couldn't believe the magnificent book had been buried in chest under some trees and still survived intact.

Donovan's expert pointed to the other books on the table, six in all. He explained that the chest must have been commissioned for its purpose as all the books looked to be in good order. "And they're all originals too, it's incredible."

"This one looks very familiar," said Carrie, pointing to a green leather-bound book. "Isn't that similar to the one found beside Ambrose?"

The book expert nodded again. "Yes, and the one by the second body. Still trying to identify it though, it isn't familiar to me. However, my estimate would be that the contents of that chest would be worth in and around fifteen million euro. With most of that being the Book of Hours – the Rothschild Prayerbook."

Carrie gasped. Oldchurch had never had a find of such magnitude, but what did it all mean? She looked over at Ellen, who was making copious notes in her book.

The Secrets of Beacon Court

"I think we need to make a visit to Beacon Court – what d'you think Carrie?" she asked, heading for the door without waiting for an answer. Carrie took a last look at the books on the table and followed her boss out of the room.

While they were driving, Ellen filled Carrie in on her theory so far. "It must be obvious to you by now that we've stumbled on something more than just murder here. Personally, I haven't ever dealt with anything like this, but I do have some other information, which I'll share when I have it confirmed." She looked across at Carrie, who seemed to be a bit relieved that her boss was feeling as overwhelmed as she was. "I believe we have Ambrose Finnegan and Jimmy Hennessey dealing in rare books, but they are keeping some originals and selling copies – hence the copies of the book we found by each body. The question is are the twins involved?"

Carrie replied instinctively "Yes, I think they have to be. I'm not entirely sure all four of them were working 'together' though. I get the distinct impression that the girls were trying to get rid of the boys, and vice versa."

"I'm not sure how it all worked yet, but I think the answer is within those four walls. Let's start with Peter Portius. I have a feeling there is more to him than meets the eye," said Ellen.

When she knocked on Portius's door, it opened almost immediately. They were ushered in, and were very surprised to find Lucien, the postman, also in the flat. Carrie looked over to Ellen and raised her eyebrows, they hadn't seen this coming.

"Thank God you two are here," said Peter, showing them to seats and taking a chair by the window for himself. "Lucien, you fill them in, I'll keep an eye out."

Lucien nodded, and was amused by the confusion on the faces of both detectives. "We have a lot to tell you," he said, "starting about two years ago …"

For the next hour Lucien, Peter, Ellen and Carrie, discussed drugs cartels, illegal book trading, possible human trafficking … and murder; a lot to take in; and questions were fired by the detectives seeking clarity and corroboration.

"So that takes us up to the recent events," said Peter. "We don't believe Ambrose blew our cover, we think he was going to jump ship and give us everything he had on the whole scheme. It was just too late, somebody found out he was planning to double cross them, we just don't know who."

"Yes," said Lucien, "we had suspected Jimmy. We knew he wasn't keen on Ambrose being the boss and leaving him playing second fiddle. Then your lot found him dead, so bang went that theory. The chest is interesting though, and the fact that you've found the Book of Hours - incredible!"

"So, what about the twins then? I can't see it myself, but have you any theory on either of them?" Carrie asked.

"Don't think either of them are killers, you're right there," said Peter. He scratched his head and rubbed the stubble along his jaw. "They were never going to let the boys take control, they just wanted them there as cover. I know Angela was fed up with Ambrose, and I also know she's been doing the dirty on him with Salinger. Caught her sneaking out of his apartment a couple of times now."

"We know he's the money man," said Lucien. "He's in a load of bother though; I reckon he's lost the cartel a bundle and he's getting ready to bolt. He's been meeting your boss a lot too."

Ellen held up her hand. "I know about all that," she said, turning to Carrie to explain. "I'm sorry, Carrie, but the Chief Super briefed me before I started in Oldchurch. He said there were a few officers I'd need to keep an eye on, they've had doubts about Downes for a while. I wasn't supposed to discuss this with anyone ...so keep it to yourself ...right?'

"I knew something was up," she said to them, "but what puzzles me is how unsurprised I am to hear it confirmed. Do you think he was in on all this too?"

"We don't think so," said Lucian "he's not a good enough actor to play both sides. He knew Salinger was playing with dodgy money, but we're confident Downes was only trying to line his own pockets for his retirement. There may have been an element of blackmail, and he certainly had run ins with Jimmy Hennessey, but it was all about himself, he only thought about number 1 – Downes."

"Right," said Ellen, stretching out her back. "We need to get moving. With all your undercover intel and with what we've gleaned ourselves, we've ruled out both twins and Salinger, yes?" She looked around the group, and they nodded their agreement. "What's your feeling on the other residents then? What about Effie Boyle?"

Everyone looked to Peter Portius. "Well Effie is a nutcase," he said simply. "She's invested with Salinger, yes, but she has so much coming in from her trust fund I don't think the odd grand here or there is an issue.

She likes to think she's living on the edge, but it's all in her head really."

"It's not her." Lucien smiled around the room. "She has a soft spot for me, I've spent some time with her, sounding her out. Peter is right, she's harmless, unless you're trying to escape her amorous clutches!"

"Right. Who's next then?" asked Carrie. "I'm thinking that Geraldine Haven is more of an amateur sleuth than a murderer?"

"You're very astute, D.S. King," replied Peter, impressed that the gardai were more up to speed than he had given them credit for. "She has invested in Salinger too, but I think it was more of a test really. She knows something is going on here, but I'd be pretty confident she hasn't any clue as to the scale of the crimes she has almost got herself embroiled in. I think her time with the DOJ has given her ideas above her pay grade."

"Now we're coming to our prime suspects then. I think I'm happy enough that we have all come to the same conclusion, so we can take it from here." Ellen looked across at Carrie, who nodded in agreement. "We'll wrap up the case for the murders, and we'll then liaise with you when you have the last pieces of the jigsaw on the Salinger/Twins cartel activity. That part is above our own pay grade – but we'd appreciate being kept in the loop."

"Agreed," replied Peter, with Lucien nodding his assent. "I'll get on to Interpol, and Lucien, you'll contact your people? We could have this done by the end of the week. Finally!" He couldn't believe retirement was imminent, now all he needed was the apartment in Old Connaught House, that would be the icing on the cake.

"Well Carrie," said Ellen, "I think the next stop is Primrose Hill Nursing home, don't you?"

Carrie agreed and the two detectives made their way out to their car.

Twenty minutes later, having spoken to the head of operations at the nursing home, they were heading for the room of Rory Carthusian. Apparently, he

205

didn't mix much with the other residents, due to his "dementia" and stayed mainly in his own room. Ellen knocked on the door and walked in Rory Carthusian was caught red handed with a cigar and what looked like a glass of whiskey almost up to his lips.

"What the bloody hell?" he looked angrily at them, shocked by their sudden appearance. Then he remembered he was supposed to be suffering from dementia and shook himself back into the part.

"Just in time, the bar has just opened, it's so good of you to come." He said, "I love this club, don't you? Always have the best whiskey on tap. Now remind me, when did we last meet?" He looked innocently up at the two detectives.

"Right, Rory, we know all about you and your "dementia", we're not here to pull you out of your luxurious

The Secrets of Beacon Court

surroundings, we just want answers," said Ellen. She was determined to get to the bottom of everything and wasn't going to leave without every detail revealed to her.

Rory could obviously read all of this in her face. He visibly sagged, and then shook with genuine fear. "If I tell you, what'll happen to me? I want protection!"

"We know what you've been up to Rory, so you may as well come clean." Said Carrie sitting down and taking out her notebook, pen ready.

Rory sighed, stubbed out his cigar and took a swig of whiskey as he noted the surprised look on their faces.

"Well, it's six o'clock somewhere in the world!" he said, putting the glass down and sitting back more comfortably.

"Now ... that this information came from me can't go beyond these four walls or I say nothing at all."

"We've OK'd that with the boss; go ahead and speak."

"Tell me what you know so far,' he said, "I will only confirm if you are right, I won't actually give you any *new* information. That gives me some protection."

"Right," Ellen replied, taking out her own notebook. "Sorry Carrie, I had this information confirmed by the Chief Super late last night, I couldn't fill you in until we had spoken to Rory."

Carrie shrugged her shoulders, she had known there was more going on than she was in on, but that was a D.I.'s job, not hers.

"Ok, Rory." Ellen continued. "We know that your wife's murder was not an accident. We also know that your family has been involved in laundering drug money for a number of years, and that you have funded your lifestyle by dealing in stolen rare books. You used that money to pay for a lifetime of care here. All correct so far?"

Rory nodded again.

"We suspect that you have been keeping an eye on the goings on at Beacon Court?"

Once more Rory just nodded.

"And you're having a relationship with … "

Rory held up his hand. "No names, please," he said, looking furtively around the room as if he suspected someone was listening in. "You're correct, but I must protect my partner."

"Fair enough," replied Ellen. "So, this 'partner' has been keeping you in the loop by pretending to have no idea what the twins and their boyfriends are up to. She is at huge personal risk right now, so we need to keep her safe. Can you contact her and tell her we'll send a team to Beacon Court this afternoon? We're going there now to make the arrest, once your partner is in safe hands."

"Do you really think she's at risk? I can't lose her; I can't go through that heart ache again. Please, please, keep her safe, don't let that woman anywhere near her, please!" Rory implored.

"You are aware of who the murderer is then?" Ellen asked, and Rory nodded in reply. "Call her now; we'll head to the house."

As Ellen and Carrie rose to leave, Rory grabbed his glass with a shaking hand, took a deep drink, and picked up his phone.

"Right, Carrie, what do I need to confirm before we get back to Beacon Court? Are you up to speed?" Ellen looked across at Carrie, giving her a moment to collect her thoughts.

"I think I know now who our killer is, I hadn't realized Rory was still involved, but it all makes sense now, when you go back over all the information we have." Carrie said, proving that she was every bit as sharp as Ellen had suspected. This boded well for their future working relationship.

Back at Beacon Court, the two detectives made their way into the building.

"Afternoon, Bunty," they called over to the cleaner, who was dusting down the bookshelves in the hall, and humming tunelessly.

"Ladies," said Bunty as she stopped humming and turned to watch them climb the stairs up to the first floor. "Hmm, now where are those two off to?"

When they got to Kitty's door they knocked. It was immediately opened a tiny crack, allowing an eye to peer out at them. "Oh, thank goodness it's you! I've been beside myself since Rory called."

Kitty opened the door and ushered the two women inside. "We need to get you to safety, Kitty," said Ellen said. "We have a team en-route, but you must stay here in the apartment until they arrive."

The Secrets of Beacon Court

Kitty had met Rory at one of her seances, he had been trying to make contact with his late wife.

Although heartbroken and terrified at that time in his life, he had fallen for Kitty hook, line and sinker. He had tried to keep away from her, fearing for her safety, but she pursued him and, in the end, they began an affair which they kept secret from everyone, despite all the dangers.

She had been his eyes and ears in Beacon Court, and he had been following events very closely. She and Rory had known Ambrose was a risk to everything but hadn't realized just how far he and Jimmy had been prepared to go to take over. The one thing they couldn't work out was *why* the boys had died ... couldn't work out until they followed the book trail, that is.

"We need to make our arrest, Kitty. Promise to stay here?"

Ellen and Carrie waited for Kitty to agree, and then headed out to catch a murderer.

They found Bunty coming up the stairs, hoover in hand, ready to do the landings. They waited for her to get to the top and then they stood on either side of her. Ellen began: "Bunty McGilligan, I am arresting you on suspicion of the murders of Ambrose Finnegan and Jimmy Hennessey. You do not have to say anything..." as she spoke, Carrie was putting on the cuffs.

Bunty threw back her head and laughed. So, they had found her out. She had known this day might come, but she hadn't realized how it would affect her. Her life was unravelling around her, and all she could do was laugh - maybe she could put in an insanity plea?

Later, recounting the events to the Chief Superintendent, it all became clear. Bunty had discovered the Rothschild Prayerbook when cleaning one day and knew immediately realized what it was. The next time she came back to clean, she stole the book, only to discover later when she got home that it was a fake. She was searching through Angela's apartment for the original when Ambrose came across her, and chased her out into the hall, where a scuffle broke out. Bunty grabbed a book end from the shelf and hit Ambrose. As he fell to the ground, she noticed Jimmy running across the car park and into the woods, he had a book in his hand. Bunty raced after him and, seeing it was the Prayerbook, killed him too and hid the book amongst her cleaning things. Realizing it was too late to make a getaway, she pretended to discover Ambrose's body and raised the alarm.

"I don't know why she was laughing when we arrested her," Ellen said to her colleagues afterwards. "The book she stole was forgery too, we have the real one, and it's being returned to the rightful owner. She won't be laughing when she finds that out. Plus, she's going down for a long time."

As to the Interpol/Europol joint operation into the Carthusian Empire?

Well, that's definitely another story - don't you think?

CHAPTER TWELVE

Susie Knight

Detective Inspector Ellen O'Donnell and Detective Sergeant Carrie King made their way up to Beacon Court to meet with Dr Donovan to discuss the forensic findings. They parked their car and made their way to the wooded area where the body was found.

Donovan confirmed that the 'bookend' was the murder weapon, and that it had gone to the lab for more tests on the hair and blood found upon it. He also showed them a photograph of a footprint discovered in the vicinity. It was a large, male print with a distinctive tread pattern.

He then led them to the back of the forensics van to show them the contents of the box. He opened the lid, and there they saw a beautiful, tiny, gilded book of Japanese script.

'Wow, isn't it a beautiful thing' said Carrie.

'Yes, and I would guess it is very old and worth a small fortune', said Ellen.

'We will see what we can tell you about it in due time,' Donovan replied. 'Oh yes, the word on the back of the postcard was – Aisling House'.

Ellen laughed and said 'Well, there must be a few thousand of those across Ireland. Just our luck! Thanks Dr Donovan. We will speak again soon'.

Ellen and Carrie then walked back to the house to interview Effie Boyle and Geraldine Haven about the cheques found in Jimmy's wallet. Ellen rang Effie's doorbell and when she answered the door she invited them in.

'Ms Boyle,' said Ellen, 'we have just come to ask you a few questions. As I am sure you know, Mr Hennessy has been found dead. Can you tell me why we found a cheque of yours for €1000 in his wallet?'

Effy looked uncomfortable and began twisting her hands together, 'Sean helps me with my investments,' she said, 'and he told me Jimmy would be doing something a bit unorthodox that might double my investment. I thought it was worth a try. Sean knows a lot about finance.'

'Do you know if anyone else gave him money to invest?' asked Ellen.

'Geraldine may have invested too.'

'I see ... and do you have any idea how the money was to be used?'

'No.' Effie answered. 'I don't really understand all that stuff.'

'Well ... is there anything else you can tell us?' asked Ellen.

Effie looked hesitant, 'I don't like to gossip,' she said, 'but I think Sean and Angela have been secretly spending some time together.'

'Really? Is there anything else?'

'Not that I can think of.'

'Well, thank you. If you think of anything, else please call us.'

The two guards had a similar conversation with Geraldine Haven, during which she was asked why someone who had been a solicitor would risk investing €1000 in such a reckless way.

She'd looked uncomfortable, and said that she had considered it carefully but thought it must be OK if Sean was recommending it. 'He said it was with a Japanese Investment fund that was quite complicated due to the language issues, but a great chance to make a good profit.

Once they were outside, Ellen said "So we have two men dead, a lot of Japanese connections, a male footprint and a murder weapon.

If you ask me, they are all involved in some way."

***

Superintendent Downes staggered out of the casino having lost money and having drunk one too many whiskeys.

As he rounded the corner to walk under the railway bridge, he was grabbed and dragged into a patch of rough ground held by two strong hoodlums, who were thrusting him so hard his face was rammed up against that of Conor Vaughan, a gangster well-known to the Gardai, and to Downes in particular.

'Have you sorted out that 'little problem' like you said?' Vaughan asked.

'Yes, Yes! You should have a clear run from the docks, without any checks.'

Vaughan glared menacingly at Downes and hissed, "You better be right if you want to keep your good looks! And, just to remind you we are not messing, take this." he added, stepping back and landing a punch into the Superintendent's stomach that was so hard it brought him to the ground writhing in pain.

Seconds later, with their warning heeded, the three thugs took off and were soon out of sight.

Downes, staggered to his feet and recovered himself. Then, having checked that they had gone he made his way to his car, started the engine and drove himself home to his empty house, where he let himself in, poured himself another large whiskey, and collapsed on his bed.

He woke late the next morning feeling as though he'd been hit by a train! And then, slowly he got and had a long hot shower, a cup of strong coffee, and a slice of toast. Feeling better then, he decided to visit Rory Carthusian and, having put on a suit and his very snazzy new shoes, he drove to the nursing home.

Once in Rory's room with the door firmly shut, he told Rory all that had happened. He said two Dublin gang families were lining up to move in on the smuggling racket Rory had been running, and that he was powerless to do anything to help.

Rory reckoned he might be able to fix it. But he was worried for the safety of the twins. He also reminds Downes that the 'Vaughans" were the ones who had killed his wife.

"Why don't you tell me which of them was involved; I can pass the information on, on your behalf.'

But Rory said 'No'. The fewer people who know *who* was involved the better ... and it might compromise your role in the Guards."

Downes left the nursing home then and made his way back to the station. He had a pounding headache, and a bad feeling in the pit of his stomach which had not been improved by the punch he received from Conor Vaughan!

He was hoping to get the name of the main man out of Rory … but he was clearly not going to tell … which made things very difficult for Downes for, surprisingly, he needed that name to keep the Vaughan boys happy.

Now what was he going to do?

***

Peter Portius and Lucien had arranged to have Angela and Mitzi taken to the safe house in Waterford.

The twins were visited by a woman who called herself Inspector Brady. She showed her card which identified that she was in the police protection service.

She told them that she had been asked to take them to a safe place, in case they were in any danger. Angela was grateful because she was scared! Mitzy was

225

suspicious and not so keen. She wanted to verify the situation by phoning the police.

The woman kept calm and persuaded them that the fewer people who knew, the better. She said that they must leave their phones behind, as they could be tracked. Eventually the twins agreed. They packed quickly and were driven away.

**

Peter's phone buzzed; it was a message saying that a ship was coming into Dublin Port in the early hours. His informant said he thought that there would be people on the ship that were being trafficked into Ireland and the UK, plus a big consignment of drugs.

Peter called his link in the Drug Squad and the Garda National Immigration Bureau. They had already heard about the arrival of the ship and were planning a raid. They arranged to meet at the port at midnight and wait for the ship to arrive. Peter called Lucien and they planned to make their way into the docks later that evening and find a good place to wait and observe.

At 2.24 in the morning, the ship docked. As soon as the engines were silenced the Drugs Squad moved in. All the crew and passengers were held, and the ship was searched. They found sixty foreign nationals in a container in the hold of the ship. They also found a significant amount of cocaine, cannabis and other illegal narcotics.

While the ship was being searched, another set of arrests were taking place near to the dock gates. Six members of the Vaughan Family and several associates were waiting in readiness to receive the goods. The Guards surrounded them, but they did not give in without a fight; two Guards were shot, and three gang members were injured. Another two got away.

This was a significant moment for the Gardai. They had been trying to close in on this gang for years.

Not far away a black limousine slid silently into the darkness and disappeared!

All the passengers on the ship were questioned. As well as the drugs haul, a man called Chang was found to be smuggling a consignment of rare books. He said he was to meet a woman named Robinson in the Westbury Hotel the next day at 3pm. Lucien said that he would like to see the books. He could tell that they were rare books but suspected that they were forged copies.

He took one to be forensically examined and told Chang he should meet Mrs Robinson, as arranged, and give her the books. He told Chang he would be watching from a safe distance and that after the handover he would be taken into custody along with the others.

***

Peter and Lucien made their way back to the car. It was 5.30 a.m. "What a good night," said Peter, "you wait for months and then you get the lot in one go!"

"Not quite the lot." Lucien replied with a laugh

The next day they met one of their colleagues in the Gardai; Inspector Orla Keegan. She told them that everyone was delighted at the success of the previous night and that she would accompany them to the hotel with Chang.

They had taken a good look at the books he'd been carrying. Many were Japanese, including a very rare copy of the Shin Kokin Wakash, an ancient poetry anthology. The original is priceless and is in the National Museum of Tokyo.

It is small and beautifully illustrated. However, there are a few very good copies, and these are much sort after and command a huge price tag too. This, it seemed, was one of the copies!

When Chang was brought into the room they explained what they wanted him to do and then they set off to The Westbury Hotel. Chang went into the lounge, looking for a woman wearing a red

230

beret. Seeing her he made his way to her table in a discrete corner.

He introduced himself and she told him her name was Robinson. They ordered coffee and began to talk.

After a while Chang passed her a small box. She looked inside then, nodding and smiling, she put the box in her bag and passed him a book.

Shortly after that Chang left and Peter moved over to the table and sat down. 'Hello Effie, what are you doing here?'

Effie looked shocked and couldn't think what to say. Peter continued, 'I didn't know you were into rare books? I thought that was Bunty McGilligan's thing.'

'Well … um … I sometimes help Bunty out when she is busy, and she asked me to meet Mr Chang and collect something for her today' she told him, looking flustered.

'Yes, I see ... but the problem is, Effie, that this book has been smuggled into the county and you are breaking the law'!

Just then Inspector Keegan appeared; arrested Effie for receiving stolen goods, and then rang D. I. O'Donnell at the Oldchurch Garda Station, to fill her in on developments, suggesting that Bunty McGilligan should be brought in on a charge of smuggling and receiving.

Ellen O'Donnell found Carrie King and they set off to Ashford to arrest Bunty.

On the way, Ellen filled Carrie in on recent developments. She said that they

The Secrets of Beacon Court needed to get a team into Bunty's house to look for the smuggled rare books.

'What we need to find out from Bunty, is if she knows anything about the Japanese books found with the bodies at Beacon Court?"

Carrie agreed. 'We also need to check the books in the library at Beacon Cour; Bunty may have hidden them there, and we need to examine the shoes of all the key suspects to see if we can find a match for the tread pattern we found.'

'Yes, and we need to keep that quiet, or people will start discarding their shoes,' said Ellen as they parked on the drive of Bunty's house and rang the bell.

When the door opened Ellen arrested her employing the usual caution. Bunty was shocked but, picking up her bag and phone, she went quietly out to the car.

Twenty minutes later and back in the station Inspector O'Donnell looked at Bunty. 'So, Mrs. McGilligan, you and Effie Boyle have been smuggling rare books into the country? I need you to tell me who your contacts are. What you do with the books? 'Who are your clients ? Do you make the links with the people in Japan, or do you work through someone else here?'

Bunty hesitated and then said 'Effie is not really involved; I just ask her to collect books occasionally. She knows nothing about the business.'

'Ok, I'll note that for further investigation,' said Ellen. 'But can you tell me how and why there were Japanese books beside the bodies of the murdered men at Beacon Court?'

'I don't know how they got there. They are my books. I keep a few in the

234

Library at the house. I buy and sell them, have done for years! It is normal trade. I only got involved in handling one or two rare books, under the radar.' Bunty answered, looking down at the floor.

'Well, I want you to sit and think carefully about your involvement in this affair, and the next time we talk, I want the whole truth. Do you understand?' Take her back to the cell, Sergeant.'

***

Ellen completed her notes and sat back for a moment. Superintendent Downes would be back later after having had a couple of days off … and she would need to report to him.

They had not really made much progress on the case and she was not looking forward to yet another shouting session!

At that moment she heard shouting coming from the front entrance. She picked up her phone and notebook went to see what was happening. Chief Inspector Downes was shouting. "Get me some tissue, anything. I've got dog shit all over my new shoes! Which fecking twat let his dog shit on the steps?"

Taking off his shoe he hopped up the corridor to the wash room.

Ellen looked down and froze.; she could see a perfect footprint. It was just like the one they were looking for and, while Downes was washing his hands, she photographed the print with her phone. Then she picked up the shoe and put it in an evidence bag she took form her pocket

The super had not re-appeared as far as she could see so she made for the door, put the bag in her car, and drove as fast as she could to the forensics lab where she just caught Dr Donovan as he was leaving. She showed him the shoe and the photos which he said he'd look at as quickly as possible.

She then asked him to give the information only to her, as it might compromise a colleague. He said he understood.

Once outside she thought about what this might mean. If the footprint did belong to her boss, it might mean he had killed Ambrose and Jimmy. But why? What should she do? She couldn't arrest a senior officer, could she?

She got out her phone and rang Inspector Orla Keegan at the Dublin Headquarters. She was really helpful and said she would alert GSOC. She asked Ellen to get back to her as soon as she heard from forensics. If the print was a positive match, GSOC would take over and make the arrest. Ellen closed her phone feeling relieved as she wondered if Downes might have killed Ambrose and Jimmy.

He was an angry, volatile man with a temper, so it was possible. She just hated the thought that one of her own, a superior officer, would break the law. What would make him do such a thing. She was troubled by the possibility and was not sure what to do next. It was late afternoon and she wanted to be around if a call came through from forensics. She went back to her office and tried to do some paperwork.

The phone rang.

It was Dr Donovan and he had his test results. 'I can confirm that the shoe

The Secrets of Beacon Court

print is an exact match to one found at Beacon Court.'

Ellen's stomach turned over.

"Thanks", she said, "that's very helpful."

And then she closed his call and rang Orla Keegan to tell her the news.

Keegan listened carefully and then said she would activate the GSOC team immediately.

An hour later a car arrived at the Oldchurch Garda Station. Three detectives got out and went inside. Five minutes later they re-appeared. Downes was with them as they drove off.

The unmarked car arrived at the Mountjoy Garda Station. The four men went inside. Downes was processed, and was read the caution. He was then taken into an interview room where two special branch officers - Frank Shannon and Rory Roberts from GSOC began their interrogation.

'So, how do you account for your shoe print being the same as the one found at the murder scene?' Asked Shannon.

"No comment" Downes replied.

'They are very interesting shoes. Cost a few euro, did they? I believe the sole is a new design and is not found on many shoes. Funny that the print from your shoe pattern looks to be a 100% match to the one made at Beacon Court. How do you explain that?"

"No comment."

'We have witnesses who say you were at Beacon Court that night. Is this true?"'

"No comment."

'Sean Salinger says you **were** there. He says you'd been drinking and were very aggressive. What happened? Come on why were you there?'

There was a long silence. Then Downes began to speak in a slow resigned sort of voice.

"I had invested some money with Salinger but realised he was involved in shady insider dealing so I went to the House to confront him.

When I got there, he was in Angela Carthusian's apartment. I was just trying to get them to open the door, when Ambrose came back, he opened the door with his key and went inside. Sean was only half dressed. He grabbed Sean and dragged him out into the Library. He was so mad he was clearly going to kill him so I picked up the bookend and smashed into the back of Ambrose's head to stop him.

Sean disappeared at that point and I assumed he'd gone to his apartment.

I was not wearing gloves, so had probably left prints on the bookend but did not want to touch it again, so I grabbed a book from the shelf and used it to carry the bookend out to the wood, thinking I would come back for it later.

I was about to leave, when I heard Jimmy staggering down the drive.

I lured him into the wood and hit him with the bookend too.

Then I threw the book down and went back into the house, to check if Ambrose was dead. He was.

I picked another book from the shelf and threw it down on him, so it would look like they were both killed with books. Then I left."

Rory Roberts said "We had a major success at the docks last night. We cracked a major drug and human trafficking ring. What do you know about a gang called "The Vaughans? "

Downes looked down and shook his head. "Well, of course I've heard of them. Everyone's heard of them! They are a notorious criminal family. But I have not had anything to do with them myself. "

Roberts sarcastically asked if he'd swear to it and then went on to ask about his connection to Rory Carthusian. Downes stared at him without saying anything for a moment, then said, "I know someone of that name who is in a nursing home near Bray. But he has dementia, he has been in a home for quite a few years."

Frank Shannon took over then "Do you know "Peter Portius?'

"Yes, I know who he is - a big man, he lives at Beacon Court."

'Well, he works for Interpol and he's been following a number of leads for some time. So, I put it to you again that Rory Carthusian has been running his international illegal trading business from his nursing home through Ambrose Finnegan, Jimmy Hennessy, Bunty McGilligan, Sean Salinger and you ... you Superintendent.

And I also put it to you that he was concerned that Ambrose and Jimmy were getting too powerful ... and he wanted you to sort them out? And you did sort them out!

You were all managing different parts of the business it would seem; Bunty

The Secrets of Beacon Court

McGilligan was running the rare books smuggling. She had hidden a very beautiful, forged copy of the Shin Kokin Wakash, an ancient poetry anthology, in an airtight wooden box, which she left in the wood, to be collected later. But then she was unable to retrieve it after the murder was discovered. It is apparently worth €500,000 or more!

Downes gave a slight shake of his head and then quietly said; "Effie Boyle wasn't really involved; she was just a helper for Bunty. She liked dressing up, meeting the buyers and sellers, and it helped keep Bunty's identity under wraps!"

"OK. But it looks like Salinger was involved in his own illegal financial scams and he managed to suck all of you into parting with your cash ... Angela,

Ambrose, Jimmy, Mitzi, Geraldine Haven
and you.

Lucien Poitier who, incidentally, is
also an undercover Interpol operative, was
sure you were in this up to your neck. And
he was right. But it was your shoes that
gave you away!"

CHAPTER TWELVE

Dorothea Mc Dowell

Effie, the residents thought, was a widow playing out the latter part of her life in peaceful surroundings. In fact, she was a rather gorgeous thirty something physically fit member of the socially upmarket South County Carrickmines Lawn Tennis Club. Possessing a natural gift, she easily participated in friendly organized games, both singles and doubles playing with her favourite man in club championships at the end of the season which they usually won retaining their status as best players of the year. She also represented CLTC in tournaments throughout Ireland winning several

247

trophies. She was entitled to retain two silver cups she won on three separate occasions which were concealed in her apartment deftly locked into a Queen Anne cabinet. Her passion, however, was for the leisurely game of croquet where she used her coquettish image to weave naive young men into her web purely to enhance the frivolous side of her persona whilst still enjoying the competitive edge to the game.

On alternative days Effie rose at 6.00 am and eased her red MGB GT soft top up the driveway and, as the electric gates mysteriously opened in front of her, she turned left driving a few kilometers to the leisure centre attached to the Five Star Powerscourt Hotel. She swam up and down the pool continuously for twenty minutes followed by a ten-minute soak in the jacuzzi.

The Secrets of Beacon Court

Chatting easily to her fellow members over a coffee and croissant, she then returned to her apartment where she indulged her imagination researching the lives of interesting persons on the world wide web. Effie had, in fact, never married and throughout her travels had had several lovers. Now she and Lucien, the postman, were an item both in passion and in crime.

Under the disguise of a blond wig, casual attire - albeit designer labels - lay a beautiful body of five feet eight inches, with long flowing curly brunette hair, breasts gloriously rounded, waist twenty-four inches and hips of thirty six. In other words, a perfect feminine body.

She was a RADA graduate having acted on the London theatre circuit for the previous twenty years, playing roles from a

Shakespearean to Norwegian tragedian, both to great acclaim.

Lucien, an art student prior to his Interpol life, was an adaptable and spontaneous confidante, open to Effie's devious plan. They both enjoyed sexual and gastronomical pleasures but generally abstained from overindulgence in alcohol. They enjoyed a glass of Chardonnay with dinner, and a glass of whiskey as they lay in bed.

The couple were aware of Angela's and Mitzi's penchant for debauchery and their ways of getting money by any means other than earning an honest wage. And they kept a close eye on their activities; the girls' daily lives being consumed with their passions, looking for more and more - their fragile egos never satiated. The scheming twins realized that Jimmy and Ambrose

The Secrets of Beacon Court

would mess things up for them, being too gullible, attracting the savvy of drug gangs with their loose talk and too fond of the drink which often meant they bragged about their relationship with the twins. They had to be *done in*.

Lucien and Effie hoodwinked all of the people in Beacon Court, by obtaining their trust. They managed to sell off the rare book collection, the cash from these sales and several gold bars that they found hidden in a chest were deposited in a numbered Swiss bank account. No matter how carefully a project is planned, something may still go wrong with it. The saying The *best laid schemes of mice an' men/Gang aft a-gley,* adapted from a line in *To a Mouse* by Robert Burns, aptly describes the unravelling of Effie and Lucien's murderous plans to enhance their dream of living a financially independent and easy life.

As they were driving up to the gates, they were thinking they had got away with their crime – their private jet with their trusty pilot ready on the runway in Dublin Airport to take them far far away as all hell was let loose in Beacon Court.

Rory Carthusian, father of the twins, appeared on the scene and blocked the criminals' path. Apparently, he had been only acting his dementia diagnosis and had been kept aware of every resident's activities through his cleaner and confidante, Bunty McGilligan, whose secret connection to him eventually became the downfall of the scheming lovers. It also brought their dreams of flying into the sunset to an unknown destination to continue their passionate affair crashing down in front of them. And Rory, knowing intimately the frivolity of his offspring, was not letting go of his family's long-standing reputation within the sailing and horse-riding communities surrounding the rural landscape in the locality of Beacon Court.

Angela and Mitzi had grown up there in glorious isolation, with doting parents, and nurtured by governesses until the age of 12. Then, for six years, they boarded in a posh public school in Berkshire in the lush surroundings of the English countryside where one of the royals was a fellow student.

They were not at all academic. Instead of grasping their privileged opportunities to advance their innate intelligence through science philosophy and sporting achievements, they indulged their inner needy selves by delving into the Mills and Boon world of romance gossip and intrigue. They imagined themselves living in the eighteenth century, dressed in glorious apparel attending coming out dances, hoping to catch the eye of the Prince of Wales or a handsome Duke. A world, for example, that one might watch on Netflix series. *Brigerton* was the world they truly hankered after. In other words, they never grew up to be independent mature women living a fruitful existence. They were unaware of a world where the majority of people existed in a mundane daily routine earning pittances just to house and feed themselves, bearing progeny to continue their bloodline to hopefully make this planet a better place in which to live. The twins' only goal was a life of abandon, using men like Ambrose and Jimmy, whom they could manipulate to feed their inexhaustible hunger for fun, sun and sex.

Rory, knowing the background activities of the two murderers, had informed D.I. King and D.S. O'Donnell in the Oldchurch station of the evolving situation and advised them to be at the house at a specific time. He seamlessly exposed Effie and Lucien's homicidal actions to the detectives, just as they were making their getaway in the An Post van!

On the evening prior to the events that unfolded early the following morning, Lucien had canoodled in Effie's arms scheming the minutiae of their plans to carry out the gruesome deeds. He had left his van hidden by shrubbery in the grounds of a private school not far away just as dusk was falling and sneaked into his lover's apartment, unseen by prying eyes. Having committed the second murder at around 6.00 am he casually went through the pedestrian gate and gaily strolled up the road to collect his vehicle, changing out of his tailored jacket and slacks into his uniform. He sipped a coffee from a flask in the glove compartment while breathing in fresh morning air through the open window to ease his nerves, nay, conscience. Then driving through the gates and parking in front of the mansion, he hopped out as Effie grabbed him by the elbow and … shouting out loud the rehearsed words, she dragged him into the lobby.

Looking down on the bloody body of his victim he acted out the role of an innocent man who was totally surprised at the horrific scene, ensuring the residents and then D.S.King, as Effie escorted him to his van, that he was still in shock at what he had witnessed.

A cheer went up as Lucien and Effie were manhandled into the Black Maria to take them to the 'Joy'. A Judge and Jury will decide their fate in due course. Life returned to normal – whatever normal is – in Beacon Court but one was still suspicious of any new tenant arriving on the scene with another plan to upset the residents! So, a sequel could unfold before our eyes!

CHAPTER TWELVE

Micheál MacSuibhne

Kevin Downes went bright red in the face when he saw Peter's and Lucien's warrant cards and badges. The thought of international Police forces being on his patch caused his head to spin.

He had a feeling something serious was wrong at Beacon Court, and it involved some of Ireland's top criminal organisations, but the international element was something he was going to have to get his head around.

He'd listened intently as Peter and Lucien explained what they knew, and how the two murders had prompted their superiors in Geneva and Paris to direct them to share their intelligence with the local force.

"We had no idea anyone was going to die, we thought the threat level was low but, obviously, something has changed in the past few days", Peter explained, winding up his briefing.

"I'll have to get Harcourt Square involved now I suppose", Downes said. At the back of his mind, he wondered if a successful outcome to this could mean a bigger office and, perhaps a driver.

He was shocked back to reality when heard a beep from his phone announcing the arrival of a text though. This was a great rarity; nobody would ever dare to send one if it wasn't truly serious.

He glanced at the screen and, on seeing Ellen's name, said "Here, here! What now?"

"Right lads, as we are all Police and all in this together," he told them after the phone call. "I'd like to invite you to a case conference in the Meeting Room at 3pm this afternoon. And, needless to say," he added, as he relished what was going to be shared. "you ought to stay away from Beacon Court for now."

***

"Latté darling?' Sean Salinger asked Geraldine Haven as they sat in the sun at the "Two Cafe" in Oldchurch.

"You should know better by now", Geraldine shot back through gritted teeth.

Once the waitress left them, Geraldine ripped into Sean. "What in the hell is going on? Up to last week everything was going smoothly and now we have the Gardai breathing down our necks after

Dumb and Dumber had their brains bashed in."

She had been dealing with the logistics side of the trafficking operation. Escort girls were being flown around Europe and to Russia for rich clients to do with as they wished. Through King's Inns contacts she had propagated a network of legal eagles on the continent who, under the guise of a Language School had become very successful at 'hiding in plain sight.

The money laundering part of the overall scheme was left to Sean and while he had proven to be very successful, of late things had been falling apart.

"I thought you'd be impressed by the way I was able to double our take. The forged books were top quality and nobody should have been able to tell the difference", he explained.

Geraldine was seething, as their coffee arrived. 'And then Ambrose made the unbelievable blunder of including a book of great value and its forgery, in a consignment to a bookshop in Charing Cross Road, in London. Fogg, the owner of the shop, went back over his previous orders and now claims they were all forgeries all along. They probably were!"

"You're being paranoid Ger," how could Fogg have got to the Vaughans?" Sean asked.

She couldn't believe how relaxed Sean was after the two identical murders in their collective household.

"Look, between you and me, I think Angela and Mitzi had something to do with this and London doesn't know", Sean said, with a quiver in his voice. "All we have to do is keep our heads down and carry on as we are".

***

Kevin Downes almost felt proud as he formally introduced Peter and Lucien to Ellen O'Donnell and Carrie King.

Their jaws dropped when they heard that they were faced with two international cops and not a hunky postman and a grumpy South African.

But once they had all shaken hands he got down to business and asked the D.I. and D.S. to update them on the news from the lab regarding the murder weapon and contents of the wooden chest.

"We believe we have uncovered a crime ring", O'Donnell offered.

The three men looked at each other as if to say, "Tell us something we don't know".

She went on, "The box contained junk mostly, but three books were of note. Two were almost identical. One, an original first edition print of George Eliot's *Silas Marner*, the other, a very good forgery. The third was a handwritten ledger and it contained a list of initials with figures beside them."

"Do you have any copies of pages from the ledger" Peter asked.

Carrie King opened her iPad and handed it to Peter. He and Lucien read down the list and both began to nod almost at the same time.

Downes noticed and smiled, "Do you see anything familiar gentlemen?" He asked.

Peter cleared his throat. "There's a network here which we have been trying to catch for years. If you could mail that image to my office in Geneva, they should be able to confirm what I think is going on. And if that happens, we will be able to bring down a cartel with an annual turnover running to Billions of Euro. This could stop a major route for hard drugs and a vile people trafficking network".

Lucien spoke next. "Do we know where the box with the books came from?"

"We believe it belonged to Sean Salinger,' Ellen said, 'his initials are carved into the top corner of it, beside the Stonewell College crest, which is where he boarded."

Kevin Downes seemed withdrawn; he was dying with embarrassment inside. How he had been taken for a fool by

Salinger, a man he would never wish to know. But he was and he was just going to have to get over it quickly. "So, Salinger killed Ambrose and Jimmy? And if he did, why didn't he take his old school box?"

"According to the Coroner's Report the two murders were carried out by different people. One left-handed and the other right handed they could tell from the direction of the blood spatter and the wounds themselves. The Forensics Pathologist, Margaret Blaster also says that, while Ambrose was killed by a man, Jimmy was killed by a woman".

"What a nest of vipers?" Downes commented as he got over himself.

At that moment D.S. King's phone vibrated to indicate a text message. On reading it she said, "Result! The appeal for information from the public on RTÉ Radio has been fruitful and we have very good dash cam footage of a woman climbing out over the wall of Beacon Court road frontage, from a lorry passing by at dawn of the morning Jimmy was murdered and - you're not going to believe this - it was Bunty McGilligan!"

"No wonder she was so unhelpful.". O'Donnell said. "We should pay her another visit.'

"I want you and Carrie to go and arrest Salinger immediately and bring him in for questioning. I'll head to McGilligan's with Peter and Lucien and we'll bring Bunty in. Let's tell both of them that we are arresting them for double murder, but once back here with them make sure they find out the other is also in custody too.' Downes instructed. He knew this might encourage to incriminate the other while being interviewed. It also kept him as far from Salinger as possible. "This is going to be big news for so many", Peter said to Downes. "May I suggest we have Armed Response standing by? I've authority to request it but it's your patch".

"Good thinking", Downes said as he called the control room and obtained confirmation that two ASU's would be dispatched to each of the addresses immediately. "Let's have the 'Red Stripes' make their presence felt before we make ours". He looked around the room and saw four heads nodding.

When O'Donnell and King arrived at Beacon Court the two ASU Volvo C90s really looked the part, given the way they were parked in front of the old Victorian

The Secrets of Beacon Court

house. Angela and Mitzi were at the front door as they pulled up.

"What's going on?" Mitzi asked.

"We're here to see Sean Salinger ladies, we'll get to you when we are ready", King answered as O'Donnell pushed past the twins and made for Salinger's apartment.

Through the door she could hear a man and woman arguing. She retreated to the front door and beckoned to the two armed Gardai in one of the jeeps to come in. And then she gestured to the occupants of the other jeep to go around to the side of the building where Salinger's apartment was located. Once again, she approached Salinger's apartment door and knocked three times.

A moment later she could hear his voice, "Yes, who is it?"

"It's Detective Inspector Ellen O'Donnell, Mr. Salinger, I'd like to have a word with you".

Suddenly there was a commotion inside and the sound of a window breaking. The two armed guards with O'Donnell approached the door. One kicked it in while the other provided cover with his Uzi submachine gun.

Salinger was frozen solid, with his hands up at the end of the hall.

"Don't move", O'Donnell shouted at him, "You're under arrest for murder".

Salinger's face went pale as snow and she thought he was going to faint.

As she led him to her car, the two ASU Gardai who were sent to the side of the Court came around the corner with Geraldine Haven in handcuffs. She was limping and had a bloody nose, having jumped from the first floor window.

Just as Salinger was put in the back of her car and Haven in the back of a Jeep, O'Donnell heard King call her over the walkie talkie radio.

"Can you join me in Salinger's apartment for a moment boss?"

"On my way", O'Donnell replied.

After their meeting at the Two Cafe earlier, Salinger and Haven had decided to try and identify who had been sent forged books by Ambrose and Jimmy, to see if anything could be done to prevent a backlash.

In doing so they had laid out pages of documents on Salinger's dining room table. "I'd say this will keep us busy for about a year", King said, as O'Donnell walked in.

"My God! I recognise some of these names", the DI responded as she glanced over them. Then one name caught her eye. "Holy God", she said as her eyes widened. It was none other than that of Superintendent Kevin Downes.

"Right. Let's leave one of the ASU Units here to seal this place before we can get back to it" she said, looking at King, who nodded.

***

Bunty McGilligan knew the game was up when she saw the two brightly coloured jeeps pull up at the gate of her garden. "Time for one last G and T", she thought and, as Downes' car arrived, she took a large mouthful.

The following morning Downes called a meeting with O'Donnell, King,

The Secrets of Beacon Court

Peter and Lucien, along with about a half a dozen other senior detectives from various Departments, to go over what they had confirmed at that stage.

"To begin with, I have a message from the Commissioner. He's on his way to congratulate this small team which has been involved in bringing down a criminal cartel, the likes of which he said he has never imagined possible and to offer whatever kind of support we need to begin the job of informing Europe and Interpol of the Intel we now hold". He said, beaming all round. "Good work team! And now Ellen, where are we with the murders" he asked.

O'Donnell was still unnerved at seeing the bosses name on a document found in Salingers' apartment but decided to try and put it to the back of her mind and bring it up later.

"Salinger has admitted killing Ambrose after he had discovered that he was talking to the drugs lords behind everyone's back. He was sure one of the twins would be suspected as their relationships were falling apart and as he put it "Sure, they're both completely nuts anyway".

"And Bunty McGilligan, Carrie, what can you tell us about her?" Downes asked.

"She's a real piece of work, a very evil lady" King said. "She knew the killing of Ambrose would spook Jimmy, so she hacked his Amazon Alexa account to gain access to the camera and microphone on his 'Dot' unit. She had heard his conversations with the book forgers and observed his meetings with Geraldine Haven in his lounge. Bunty had been a mole for the drugs lords for years and had funneled information and notes from conversations for years.

She also suspected that Jimmy was going to do a runner with the ledgers, so she took it upon herself to get rid of him. She got one of the dealers, Donal O'Donoghoe to arrange a meeting and knew full well that he would flee there and then. She was on the right track, as he left the Court less than an hour later. She was waiting by his car where she clobbered him to death and dragged his body into the woods. It was raining that night so she knew there wouldn't be a blood trail. She returned to the car for the wooden box but as she headed to the road, lights came on in both Angela and Mitzi's apartment at the same time. The box was too heavy to run with and she couldn't burn it in the rain so she dumped in in the woods and made for the main road. She didn't even notice the lorry driving past as she emerged onto the road." King concluded.

How Kevin Downes name ended up on a document is still a mystery.

CHAPTER TWELVE

Derek Phillips

Sean Salinger, despite the calm controlled exterior, was having the worst month of his life. Truthfully, things had not been going well for his clients including his large, key clients who resided at Beacon Court.

The Japanese Affinity Fund was in a downward trajectory with no indication that it would reverse.

Worse still, the Japanese Yen was losing value against the Euro and fast.

If that wasn't bad enough Sean had used the CFD derivatives' market to leverage up his clients' funds to the Japanese fund but at a risk. That risk was now materialising fast, and his clients had to lodge cash quickly to keep their positions open or his they would lose everything.

At least in lodging funds they could buy time. They could keep their positions open and pray the market would recover, but without available funds they could lose everything. It was an awful position to be in, the dreaded margin call.

Eighteen months earlier Salinger had been a hero with his clients, using easily available leverage through CFDs, he had doubled his clients' funds over two years. Now the gains, along with the original investments, were going down a black hole in a market where all asset classes were falling apart. Fear gripped all the international markets, and everyone was selling fast.

The Secrets of Beacon Court

There were few, if any, buyers. Sean had over two hundred clients, all were hemorrhaging losses badly, but nothing as bad as the funds that the twins had invested in, and on his advice.

Outlining the ominous position to the Carthusian twins and partners was not an easy task and set a series of actions in motion. There had been huge infighting as to who was to blame, Mitzie and Jimmy blaming Ambrose as he recommended Sean Salinger as "a fellow Stonewell student", who knew his game and had made millions." Angela too, furious with Sean's arrogant stance, had to curtail her criticism as she was in a somewhat compromised position herself with Sean. She was in no position to point a finger at Sean and none of them could. Sean had taken huge personal risks with the paperwork and money transfers to avoid anti money laundering scrutiny and he had the art dealing contact abroad to buy the books and wire the funds into the stock broking firm via offshore nominee accounts. Using a back-to-back funding mechanism, euros were lent to the twins for them to draw down, but secured indefinitely on the balances held in the off-shore nominee accounts. It was an ingenious and sophisticated arrangement. It was not the time to fall out with Sean, they had all agreed to use him and the events in the markets were outside their control. Their investment assets had taken a large hit and they would need to sell some more books, perhaps even stall the criminal gangs they owed money too. Time was a luxury they did not have, and they needed to act quickly, keep the criminal gangs on side, not spark any attention with the financial authorities or worse the Criminal Assets Bureau. They had no idea the Interpol and Europol had taken an interest in their activities or that Ambrose was nervous and considering cutting a deal to expose them, in turn for immunity by going into a witness protection program.

Having parked their in-fighting, the Carthusian's agreed that they needed Sean to sell two books through his contacts and legitimise the funds for transfer into their stockbroking account. It would take three days minimum and was risky. But Sean was not easy to track down. Of late he'd avoided being in Beacon Court. He had to escape Kitty Rae's non-stop questions about the state of her pension and the ongoing legal threats from Geraldine Haven, who would pursue every legal and financial means to get her retirement fund back to its nominal value and destroy Sean in the process.

Complicating Sean's life was the unpredictable and volatile relationship with Angela who often sought refuge late at night with him. Always in the mood for a few stiff drinks when Ambrose was out or asleep, she would arrive armed with a bottle of Vodka and an old tin box which contained an amazing array of uppers and downers. A couple of hours of alcohol fused hazy passion with Angela were enjoyable but would recede into an ambience of anxiety hostility and neurotic rants. Sean was not an active drug user but was happy to roll the joint and light it for her, to help her float out of the room giving him some peace. He may not have admitted it, but he was happy with a bit of distraction from the daily grind of updating clients with bad financial news.

He also had to avoid the hourly calls from Superintendent Kevin Downes who seemed to never tire of ranting and roaring down the phone about his lost inheritance that he had badly invested with Sean's help. "Christ" Sean thought "the man's blood pressure is inversely volatile to the stock market move ... might have to feed him with a few of Angela's hash brownies and have one day of peace".

He was due to call the Superintendent back having hung up on him two days previously. The unfortunate man was having a horrendous task reconciling his investment statement. The previous week Lehman Brothers had fallen 93% in four days and had collapsed. The little ticker symbol that Downes so happily in the past dialed into yahoo finance while it was going up had now disappeared off the screen. He was incensed. One hundred and fifty grand up in smoke. "Too big to Fail? HAAA?

Well fail it did, and you had me buy in big as it was BIG BLOODY FAILING ... AND NOW I GOT BLOODY FAILED" he roared at Sean, who was about to unleash more. Sean hung up. Worse was to come. He had got Kevin to invest his last remaining fifty grand into a new health drink called Sakashita, a Japanese quoted security that sold innovative health drinks. It's quoted share price was the same as when Kevin purchased it but it had gone through a ten for one consolidation resulting in the 1,000 shares that Kevin purchased now being replaced with 100 shares of a replacement security effectively wiping out 90% of Kevin's' investment. As the yen had depreciated against the Euro the converted investment lost further value. A fifty grand investment the previous year would now show up on Kevin's statement as being worth two thousand euro.

The staff at the Settlement desk and in Client Accounts had all received and rejected numerous calls from Kevin as Sean couldn't deal with him or the other clients which included other Beacon Court residents trying to make sense of their investments. No one at the brokerage firm could handle Superintendent Kevin Downes. No one. No one. No one.

***

As D.S. King and D.I. O'Donnell were en-route to forensics, they summarised where they were at: two murders, same approximate location and time, with the same weapon, possibly by the one person ... or was there another person involved? What was the motivation?

The initial news they got on the chest was that it contained more books and manuscripts of Asian or Arabic origin. Forensics weren't sure; they would need to get the services of an Art historian possibly one from London or Rotterdam. The detectives were still in the dark as to who were their main suspects? There was a lot they didn't know and, outside of the forensic discoveries that day, they had not a lot to update the Superintendent with. They also had made no progress with the residents in Beacon House who all seemed to avoid coming forward with information or even a convincing account of where they had been prior to the first murder, now a double murder.

King had good local knowledge. She suspected that the twins and their boyfriends and other socialites they hung out with all 'like to party' and 'party hard', but was there a hardcore criminal aspect in the house connected to other residents? King didn't think so.

It had recently been rumored that a few of the residents in the house had developed an appetite for chemical substances and were happy to exchange money openly with Ambrose or Jimmy.

Was this the reason for the cheques made out to Jimmy from Geraldine and Effie Boyle? They would need to interview them to find out. They would need to do a lot of interviewing but were they just chasing red herrings? Truth was the boys, however, rarely took payment, it was a sort of exchange for their silence and tolerance for the unusual activity in Beacon House. The boys always carried a box of their "smarties" around with them; a steady supply of Xanax, Valium and sleeping tablets, "little helpers" they described them as, which frequently brought calm or silence to Beacon House.

Peter Portius and Bunty would not take part in this arrangement and outwardly remained indifferent to it.

***

At the Forensics lab, King and O'Donnell examined the contents of the trunk. It didn't mean a lot to them. A bunch of dusty old ornate books. Yes, they would need external expert opinion but were they of value? A fact that could change things considerably.

The Secrets of Beacon Court

"Possibly it's a co-incidence that there was a collection of books in Bunty's house." O'Donnell said to King.

"Hmmm" King muttered "and she was first on the scene wasn't she?

"Or was it Sean, who knows more but chooses not to say so." stated O'Donnell.

"We could bring them in … even all of them in … we are getting nowhere."

"Let's ring the Superintendent and see if he has any objections."

The call was short and swift. The Superintendent answered the phone with one word "UPDATE?"

O'Donnell tried to brief him on the recent events when he interrupted her with a bark "I know all that, what about interviews; what did you learn? Who are

your suspects? What is your conclusion?"
he demanded.

"So, you have no suspect, and everyone now is a person of interest. I say bring them all in, including that Sack of Shite Sean Salinger, bring the lot, but keep them separate; interview them separately, and Sean Salinger … I'm looking forward to interviewing him personally "

The two detectives couldn't have known it, but the Superintendent was busy trying to find out what happened to his Japanese Investment on the Yahoo Finance page. The ticker symbol that Kevin memorized came up invalid every time he keyed it in.

Frustrated, he tried to do a search on the company name, there on the screen to his horror in black and white.

The Secrets of Beacon Court

"Sakashita is a fibrous fermented milk drink that contains the bacterial strain

Lactocantobacillus casei (LcS)

Daily consumption of Sakashita helps improve digestion through improved bowel movement and enhanced stool mass production."

Kevin read it again and again, in shock, his eyes bulging. SAKASHITA!, he rubbed his eyes, all he could see was his faint reflection on the computer monitor and the words:

S A C K. O F. S H I T A

Christ what had he invested in? A Health drink? A laxative infused with

bacteria? Well, if got his hands on Salinger
he was going to need a good dose of it by
the time he was finished with him, thought
Kevin as he put the crumpled investments
statements in his pocket.

Oldchurch Garda station that night
was a scene of total chaos as they brought
all the inhabitants of Beacon Court into the
station. Sean Salinger was only in boxer
shorts, and Angela in a skimpy gown,
having been in the midst of passion when
the Guards arrived.

Intoxicated and dazed from a
couple of joints earlier they didn't initially
take in the difficult situation they were in.

Kitty Rae had a few too many
brandies earlier, as well as two Valium, and
was in a different world, chanting and
occasionally nodding off. Effie Boyle was

heavily sedated and seemed to think she was in an airport; she kept asking where the departure gate was. Peter Portius was bringing O'Donnell up to speed on the Interpol and Europol undercover operation and how Ambrose was going to become a protected witness before being murdered.

Just then the Guards arrived in with Geraldine Haven and Mitzi Carthusian. Geraldine, incensed with the Guards inability to act on her information previously, was by then entering the same custody room as the Carthusian twins and Sean Salinger who had been actively avoiding her. Seeing him, sparked an aggressive rage and she went for him giving him one massive slap across his face, when the door sprung open and an incensed Superintendent Downes burst into the room, purple faced and panting. "Sac of Shita" he roared, as he pushed Geraldine away grabbed Salinger dragging him backwards into his office.

The sight of Sean being hauled across the floor with his boxer shorts sliding off silenced the room and they all watched in shock as Downes stuffed the crumpled statements into Salinger's mouth. "Digest that now … ya too big to fail sac of shita "he roared.

***

O'Donnell had to stop her interview with Peter Portius to intervene with Downes before he went too far and suffocated one of their key suspects. "Superintendent stop." She screamed "We need him alive. There's a lot you need to be brought up to speed on and we need you in the next room."

The Secrets of Beacon Court

Kevin composed himself and left Sean on the floor of his office spluttering and coughing up half digested investment statements.

"Jesus, Superintendent," said O'Donnell, "Interpol have undercover people working inside the house.

We've one of their operatives in my office right now filling me in. This case is now huge and part of an international drugs and criminal ring. And what are you doing with Sean? He's not the murderer." she gasped.

Just then King arrived; bringing in Bunty and her husband. "We need their house searched, she stated, a little out of breath. "there could also be more valuable books there."

"Bunty's hardly committed a double homicide" roared Downes.

"No," King replied, suppressing a grin, "there is a new angle on this, Rory Carthusian, the twins Dad, ... has disappeared without a trace ... gone ... and he probably has the most valuable book of the lot with him.

Keep turning the page to find the list of alternative denouement authors

Lotta Vokes

The Secrets of Beacon Court

The 'co-writing' format used in this book was devised by Alan Grainger who got his idea from the Victorian children's game of Consequences. He wrote the prologue, and the other chapters were written by the authors, listed below, in the order of their inclusion in the book.

Edel O'Kennedy (Chapter One)

Susie Knight (Chapter Two)

Dorothea McDowell (Chapter Three)

Annie Devine (Chapter Four)

˙ Derek Phillips (Chapter Five)

Natalie Cox (Chapter Six)

Emma Parker (Chapter Seven)

Jane Durston (Chapter Eight)

Micheál MacSuibhne (Chapter Nine)

Mary Cait Hermon (Chapter Ten)

Edel O'Kennedy and Susie Knight did the editing

Mike and Jane McDonnell selected the denouement

Lotta Vokes

The Secrets of Beacon Court

This is a book of fiction

The people in the story, and most of the
businesses, are imagined though they may sound
familiar. Any resemblance to a real person is
coincidental and should be ignored.

The same is not quite true for places; Beacon
Court, is entirely fictional as is Bunty's cottage and
Rory's accommodation in Dundrum, but quite a
few of the other locations exist.

Published by Charlotte Vokes

(aka Alan Grainger)

Lotta Vokes

Printed in Great Britain
by Amazon